THE AUTHORIZED ILLUSTRATED BOOK OF
ROGER ZELAZNY
ILLUSTRATED IN FULL-COLOR BY
GRAY MORROW

SHADOWJACK
an all-new fantasy with the medieval anti-hero

AN AMBER TAPESTRY
epic murals based on Corwin and the Amber worlds

A ROSE FOR ECCLESIASTES
the first graphic story version of the fantasy classic

THE DOORS OF HIS FACE, THE LAMPS OF HIS MOUTH
an illustrated adaptation of the Nebula award story

A ZELAZNY TAPESTRY
key scenes from the Zelazny novels

THE FURIES
a dark chase over four worlds — a graphic fantasy

edited and adapted by
BYRON PREISS

PUBLISHED BY
BARONET PUBLISHING COMPANY
NEW YORK
PRODUCED BY
BYRON PREISS VISUAL PUBLICATIONS, INC.

Acknowledgments

This book has been produced with the support of Roger Zelazny and his agent, Henry Morrison. To them both, our sincere appreciation.

The Illustrated Roger Zelazny © 1978 Byron Preiss Visual Publications, Inc.

The Doors of His Face, the Lamps of His Mouth has been previewed in *Star-Reach* publications. For issues of Star-Reach, contact Bud Plant, Box 1668 Grass Valley, California 95945. Published by Mike Friedrich, P.O. Box 385 Hayward, CA.

A Rose for Ecclesiastes has been previewed in the January, 1978 issue of *Heavy Metal* Magazine.

An Amber Tapestry has been previewed in *Mediascene* ($1.50) Box 974, Reading, PA.

The graphic story versions of *Rock Collector, The Furies, The Doors of His Face, A Rose for Ecclesiates, Shadowjack* and all illustrations © 1978 Byron Preiss Visual Publications, Inc.

Original story, *The Furies* © 1969 Roger Zelazny; Original story, *A Rose for Ecclesiastes* © 1971 Roger Zelazny; Original story, *Rock Collector* © 1970 Roger Zelazny; Original Story *Shadowjack* © 1978 Roger Zelazny; Original Story, *The Doors of His Face* © 1971 Roger Zelazny. These stories originally appeared in *Galaxy*, The *Magazine of F. and S.F.*

Color art for *Shadowjack* by Stephen Oliff
"The Furies" logo by Alex Jay.
Preliminary drawings and pencil art for *The Furies* by Michael Goldin. All other art by Gray Morrow.

Front Cover logo and design by William Murphy.

Graphic story design by Byron Preiss.

For information on subsidiary rights contact The Sterling Lord Agency, 660 Madison Avenue, New York, New York.

A limited, numbered and signed hardcover edition of this book is available for $14.95 & 95¢ postage from Baronet Publishing Company, 509 Madison Avenue, New York City.

Mechanicals by Basile Associates.

Special thanks to Joan Brandt, Jim Steranko, Norman Goldfind, Sean Kelly, Jack's finger and, of course, Gray Morrow.

ISBN: 0-89437-014-6

First Baronet Edition Published February, 1978

Send all comments to Byron Preiss Visual Publications, Inc., 680 Fifth Ave., N.Y., N.Y. 10019.

Introduction

What you hold in your hand is nothing less than a ground-breaking experiment in graphic science fiction. Each of the five fantasies in this book are developed in a different way. At least two systems of graphic storytelling have never been seen before in this country.

The Illustrated Zelazny is a high quality effort to move the framework and focus of the graphic story in new and more sophisticated directions. At the same time, this book is intended to be *fun* for the reader. Hopefully you'll get a kick out of the visual tricks played within it.

With the exception of "Shadowjack," an original story scripted just for the book, all of the tales here are well-loved Roger Zelazny standards. "A Rose for Ecclesiastes," which Gray Morrow has illustrated in magnificent color, is an intricate and sensitive fantasy about the first Earth poet on Mars. "The Doors of His Face" is an adventurous tour de force, an epic sea hunt on another planet "The Furies" is Roger's hat trick; philosophical, mythical and straight heroic fantasy mingled with four very different yet strangely sympathetic charcters. Ted Sturgeon has said it leaves you "gasping with a fable in your hands."

Both Roger and Gray possess a special sense of the fantastic. If the work in this book doesn't leave you gasping, then at least you'll laugh, smile or nod your head with an enthusiastic "Yeah!" So be prepared for over 60 pages of color and a score of sensational black-and-white.

A final word or twelve about the storytelling herein. The type is meant to be read in columns, as if in a newspaper. Read one column at a time, north to south. Read columns in sequence, from left to right. The illustrations are integrated into this scanning pattern.

Zelazny fanatics will be pleased to find new comments by the author about his work scattered throughout the book. Roger has sanctioned the deletions made in his tales. Much of the "adaptation" work has been done for the sake of visual space.

The illustrated adventure begins on the next page. We look forward to your comments in our New York office.

This story precedes the action in my novel *Jack of Shadows*. The world on which it is set is distinctive in that one side of it constantly faces its sun. This daylight side is ruled by the laws of science, and giant energy screens keep the population from frying and the land from being baked dry. The dark side, where the laws of magic hold sway, is preserved from the cold by a sorcerous matrix of perpetually renewed spells. The two realms have little contact with one another, though they figure prominently in each other's myths, folklore and legends.

Many of the darksiders possess idiosyncratic supernatural abilities, which are stronger or weaker in various locales. When one such individual finds a spot where his powers are at their highest he realizes this to be his special place of power and makes every effort to gain political and military control, to establish his own kingdom there. This may of course require considerable time and effort, for the territory may overlap with that of another sorcerous power.

But the darksiders possess time for considerable effort, in that each of them is endowed with more than one life—just how many per, being a closely guarded secret with each individual. Some time after dying, such a one finds himself strangely resurrected, naked, in the Dung Pits of Glyve at the world's darkest pole. This necessitates a perilous journey back to more congenial climes for whatever endeavor was underway there.

Jack, Jack of Shadows or Shadowjack, as he is variously known, is neither a darksider nor a daysider, but a creature of twilight, having been born in the gray area between the two realms. His power is not dependent upon place, but upon the presence of shadows, with which he has a magical affinity. Like the darksiders, he is possessed of more than one life and no desire to squander any of them. Unlike the darksiders, he is free to rove the dark realms, his powers seemingly undiminished; and because of his trade—thievery—considerable travel is generally necessary.

This story, set early in his career, brings him in contact with other darksiders in their places of power, where he must pit his cunning and his shadow-force against them.

SHADOW JACK

My images darted within that place—but the place was not all that large, and the shadow itself was wavering as their wings beat above me, partly blocking a dim light from the castle . . .

. . . and there were too many of them. Enough to strike at each flickering Jack and the one substantial one. When the arms I could not avoid came at me, I let go my images and drew the remaining force the shadows had lent me back into myself.

I have always preferred stealth to violence. It is indecent to be outweighed, outnumbered and still have to fight. Violence, like disease or a bad debt, is better to give than receive.

"I've a mind to accept your apology," I told her, "since I, too, had a few visions enroute. They are exceeded however, in an unexpectedly pleasant direction."

"I am Vara Lylyra," she said, bidding her stony sentinels return to their niches. "This is my place of power. I detected your approach but recently, and had to move quickly."

"Come," she continued, "I will show you about. There are certain matters I wish to discuss."

The tour eventually took us to her bedchamber, and I wondered as to priorities—discussion first, or—?

"I require the services of the very finest thief available," she said, "to steal for me the Eye of Iskat."

"Oh?" I said, as she moved nearer, flame and sword-metal masked by perfume and softness. "What is the Eye of Iskat?"

"It is a gem of wondrous potency," she replied. "It enhances one's natural powers enormously. It is currently in the possession of Lord Belring of the Corners. He keeps it in his Court of the Hundred Towers. Do you know it?"

"I have heard of it," I replied. "Each tower is said to contain a bell which begins ringing if someone sets a foot within it. An effective system."

"Yes, that is the place," she said, moving even nearer. "I would like you to go there and fetch it for me."

"I have also heard something about a guardian in that place . . ."

"True," she said, embracing me lightly. "The old sorceror has created some sort of brittle beast-man called the Vorkle. It tends to be somewhat transparent and difficult to see. But you, of course, are now forewarned . . ."

"The jewel is hidden in one of the towers?"

"I believe so, though I cannot tell which."

Whenever I am spoken of in shadow, I know what is said... In the shadowy confines of her chamber, Vara regarded me in her crystal and muttered her displeasure at the faithlessness of men. Then her eyes grew bright. "A döppelgänger!" she said, clapping her hands. "I will send his double—with all his skills and none of his mischief!"

It would be identical to me in physical respects, though lacking those charming intangibles which make me what I am. I worried within my fetters of light. I could begin to fade as it exerted itself, lapsing finally into total nothingness...

As she charged it with the errand I had declined, I realized that I would have to escape soon...

Then she began a fresh spell, and I felt a pang in my breast as she did so. This was dangerous magic indeed—for the duplicated. The longer a döppelgänger exists, the weaker his principal becomes, until finally...

...I would have to escape, pursue it and be merged with it...

As it tore off through the night, heading for the Court of the Hundred Towers, I hit upon a dangerous course of action. I struggled to recall the spell Vara had used to bind me... It came back to me then, and I rehearsed it in my mind. I knew of no way to diminish the light-bands...

...But I might be able to overload the spell by reinvoking it.

Weak, though... I was very weak as I rushed from that place and made my way out of the castle.

The gargoyles sought me, but I had already reached a well-shadowed vicinity. None could find me there against my will.

When they finally gave up, I continued on my way toward The Corners—a place where several kingdoms abut—near where Lord Belring holds his court. Weakening with every league, I struggled to make haste, wondering how my döppelgänger was faring in the court of the bells...

Monolithic, I regarded the heaped campaniles of the court, the great bells visible in many of them. Most were still, but a few had begun ringing, indicating that my double had commenced his search among the towers. I hurried ahead.

Somewhere within that place was the other Jack, and I had to find him before the Vorkle did—find him, while avoiding the Vorkle myself—and figure a way to achieve our merger. Another bell began pealing as I made my way into the court. I scanned the skyline in that direction and caught a glimpse of a figure strangely like myself leaping from one tower to another...

BONG!

BONG!

I drew the shadows about me like an extra cloak and released them again. They spread about the room, image after image of myself, each fleeing, dancing, darting in a different direction. For a moment, the Vorkle stood like an ice sculpture, baffled at the display. But then he moved, turning—first one way, then another—flailing his arms, reaching out, grasping after, seeking to destroy one of my images after another. The huge bell swung to and fro, its peals deafening me to any noise the creature might be making.

I moved my images faster and faster, twisting, spinning, tumbling before him, about him. He turned and turned, seeming to grow more bewildered with each pass. Between the pealing and this action, however, I felt my strength begin to wane once again. Was I—the real me—becoming as transparent as this creature I faced?

As I regarded the creature's remains, the skin on my neck crawled, as though I, myself, might at that moment be an object of scrutiny . . . and why not? My double was somewhere near, and the mad lord of this place could hardly be unaware of what had transpired.

If Belring had seen the destruction of his guardian, he would doubtless be heading to brew some new mischief.

As a mumbler, a curser, he was first-class. I heard my name both in his musings and in the spell which followed. His magic troubled me more than a little . . .

I had a picture of him as he had been described to me—stocky and strong. If just a few minutes of his music had affected my mind so, I wondered what they might have done to his, over the years.

Within a smoky mirror he conjured up my form, his warped sense of humor doubtless drawing delight from the compounding of my difficulties. No true döppelgänger this lethal image, however. The new double was formed of elements which would prove instantly fatal to me were I to merge with it rather than the one I sought . . .

AN AMBER TAPESTRY

**NINE PRINCES IN AMBER
THE GUNS OF AVALON
SIGN OF THE UNICORN
THE HAND OF OBERON**

I began the Amber series about a decade ago with *Nine Princes in Amber* and, with time out in between to write other things, continued the tale through the remaining books necessary to take it where it was going; to wit, *The Guns of Avalon, Sign of the Unicorn, The Hand of Oberon* and *The Courts of Chaos,* in that order.

My narrator is Corwin, one of the nine princes of Amber. Opening on Earth, with his recovery from an auto accident, the story takes Corwin through the beginnings of recovery from the centuries' long amnesia which had sealed his exile from Amber, the real world, of which others are but shadows. Tricking on-the-scene relatives into believing that he is fully recovered, Corwin persuades his brother Random to take him back to Amber. After a perilous journey through Shadow, they are hunted by their brother Julian in the great Forest of Arden.

Later, confessing the true state of his memory to Random and their sister Dierdre, he takes their advice and flees with them to Rebma, the city beneath the sea, a mirror-image of Amber beneath the ocean's waters. There, it is suggested, he walk the image of the great Pattern of Amber, an experience which may restore his memory in full, up to and including the recollection of his power over Shadow. This power grants to one of the blood of Amber the ability to traverse the shadow worlds—a possible infinity of variously distorted images of Amber herself.

Corwin learns that the throne of Amber is currently under the protection of his elder brother Eric, in the absence of their father, Oberon. Eric has apparently decided that their father will not be returning, and is beginning preparations to have himself crowned King of Amber. There had long been dispute over the succession to the throne, and Corwin feels his claim to it is more valid than Eric's. He determines to dispute the matter.

Corwin's brothers are Random, Eric, Bleys, Brand, Caine, Gerard, who is Master of the Fleet, Julian, Master of Arden, and Benedict, Defender. His sisters are Dierdre, Florimel, Fiona and Llewella. The family maintains contact with one another over great distances by means of special sets of cards, Tarot-like decks in which they all figure as Trumps. These versatile pasteboards—designed by Dworkin, a shadowy figure who had been an advisor to Oberon—also provide instantaneous transportation for any parties concerned.

Corwin quickly discovers that he has returned at a bad time; but, true to his nature and nurture, he determines to make the most of it, come magic, plotting, fratricide or war. Things grow more complicated as the action advances.

I had grown up reading the science fiction of the thirties and the forties (old magazines being available and cheap), and I had a strong sentimental attachment to what is now called "space opera." For as far back as I can remember, I had wanted to write stories—and I had long wanted to do something of that sort. When I began selling fiction in the early sixties it was too late—almost. The space program had already invalidated the Mars and Venus of Edgar Rice Burroughs and his spiritual successors—almost. I decided that if I were going to try anything of that sort it had to be right away. If I wanted to do homage to those forces which had helped to shape me as a writer, if I wanted to pay tribute to Weinbaum and Kuttner and countless others, if I wanted to depict a dying red world and a Martian priestess or a monster in the stormy seas of Venus I would have to act quickly and do my best. I knew that I would only be allowed one shot at each world, and then I would have to leave the solar system. "A Rose for Ecclesiastes" was my only word on Mars, "The Doors of His Face, The Lamps of His Mouth" all that I would have to say on Venus. So I did it. I wrote them both and I got in under the wire. "Rose" came first, and because I was, in a very real way, saying good-bye to a whole class of stories, I felt that I might as well throw in everything but the Martian kitchen sink. I am glad that I did. I will never be able to write another story like this again. Then, it could still be called science fiction. Now, it must be read as fantasy. Either way, there's the story.

A ROSE FOR ECCLESIASTES

I was busy translating one of my *Madrigals Macabre* into Martian on the morning I was found acceptable. The intercom had buzzed briefly, and I dropped my pencil and flipped on the toggle in a single motion.

"Mister G," piped Morton's youthful contralto into the speaker, "the old man says I should 'get hold of that damned conceited rhymer' right away, and send him to his cabin. Since you're the only damned conceited rhymer . . ."

"Let not ambition mock thy useful toil." I cut him off.

So, the Martians had finally made up their minds!

The entire month's anticipation tried hard to crowd itself into the moment, but could not quite make it. I was frightened to walk those forty feet and hear Emory say the words; and that feeling elbowed the other one into the background.

So I finished the stanza I was translating before I got up. It took only a moment to reach Emory's door. I knocked twice, just as he growled, "Come in."

"You wanted to see me?"

"That was fast. What did you do, run?"

Little fatty flecks beneath pale eyes, thinning hair, and an Irish nose; a voice a decibel louder than anyone else's . . . .

Hamlet to Claudius: "I was working."

"Hah!" he snorted. "Come off it. No one's ever seen you do any of that stuff."

I shrugged my shoulders and started to rise.

"Sit down!" He stood up.

He walked around his desk. He hovered above me and glared down. (A hard trick, even when I'm in a low chair.)

"You are undoubtedly the most antagonistic bastard I've ever had to work with! I'm willing to admit you're smart, maybe even a genius, but—oh, hell!"

He made a heaving gesture with both hands and walked back to his chair. "Betty has finally talked them into letting you go in. Draw one of the jeepsters after lunch."

I nodded, got to my feet. My hand was on the doorknob when he said: "I don't have to tell you how important this is. Don't treat them the way you treat us."

I closed the door behind me.

I was nervous, but I knew instinctively that I wouldn't muff it. My Boston publishers expected a Martian Idyll, or at least a Saint-Exupéry job on space flight. The National Science Association wanted a complete report on the Rise and Fall of the Martian Empire. I knew they would both be pleased.

I made my way to our car barn, drew one jeepster and headed it toward Tirellian.

Flames of sand, lousy with iron oxide, set fire to the buggy. They swarmed over the open top and bit through my scarf; they set to work pitting my goggles.

Suddenly I was heading uphill, and I shifted gears to accommodate the engine's braying. I reached the crest of the hill, I had raised too much dust to see what was ahead but I have a head full of maps, so I bore to the left and downhill, adjusting the throttle. I rounded a rock pagoda and arrived. Betty waved as I crunched to a halt, then jumped down.

"Hi," I choked, unwinding my scarf. Where do I go and who do I see?"

I looked at her chocolate-bar eyes and perfect teeth, at her sun-bleached hair, close-cropped to the head and decided that she was in love with me.

"Mr. Gallinger, the Matriarch is waiting inside to be introduced. She has consented to open the Temple records for your study." She paused here to pat her hair. Did my gaze make her nervous?

"They are religious documents, as well as their only history," she continued, "sort of like the Mahabharata. She expects you to observe certain rituals in handling them, like repeating the sacred words when you turn pages—she will teach you the system."

I nodded quickly, several times.

"Uh—" She paused. "Do not forget their Eleven Forms of Politeness and Degree. They take matters of form quite seriously—and do not get into any discussions over the equality of the sexes—"

"I know all about their taboos," I broke in. "Don't worry. I've lived in the Orient, remember?"

She dropped her eyes and seized my hand. "It will look better if I enter leading you."

I swallowed my comments, and went inside.

The Matriarch, M'Cwyie, was short, white-haired, fiftyish, and dressed like a Gypsy queen. Accepting my obeisances, she regarded me as an owl might a rabbit. The lids of those black eyes jumped as she discovered my perfect accent. "You are the poet?"

"Yes," I replied.

She turned to Betty. "You may go now."

Betty muttered the parting formalities, gave me a strange sidewise look, and was gone. She apparently had expected to stay and "assist" me. But I was the Schliemann at this Troy, and there would be one name on the Association report!

M'Cwyie rose. "Our records are very, very old," she began. "Your word for their age is 'millennia.'"

"I'm very eager to see them."

"We will have to go into the Temple—they may not be removed."

I was wary. "You have no objections to my copying them, do you?"

"No. I see that you respect them, or your desire would not be so great."

"Excellent." She seemed amused. I asked her what was funny.

"The High Tongue may not be so easy for a foreigner to learn."

It came through fast. No one on the first expedition had gotten this close. I had had no way of knowing that this was a double-language deal—a classical as well as a vulgar. I knew some of the Prakrit, now I had to learn all their Sanskrit. "Ouch! and damn!"

"Pardon, please?"

"It's non translatable, M'Cwyie. But imagine yourself having to learn the High Tongue in a hurry, and you can guess at the sentiment."

She seemed amused again, and told me to remove my shoes. She guided me through an alcove . . .

. . . and into a burst of brilliance!

"Sir," he had said, "I'd sort of like to study on my own for a year or so, and then take pre-theology courses at some liberal arts university. I feel I'm still sort of young to try a seminary, straight off."

"But you have the gift of tongues, my son. You were born to be a missionary. You say you are young, but time is rushing by you like a whirlwind. Start early."

I can't see his face now; I never can. Maybe it is because I was always afraid to look at it then.

Years later, when he was dead, I looked at him and did not recognize him.

We had met nine months before my birth, this stranger and I. He had never been cruel—stern, demanding, with contempt for everyone's shortcomings—but never cruel. He had tolerated my three years at St. John's, possibly because of its name, never knowing how liberal and delightful a place it really was.

But I never knew him, the man atop the catafalque demanded nothing now; I was free not to preach the Word. But now I wanted to, in a different way.

I did not return for my senior year in the fall. I had a small inheritance coming, and a bit of trouble getting control of it, since I was still under eighteen. But I managed.

It was Greenwich Village I finally settled upon.

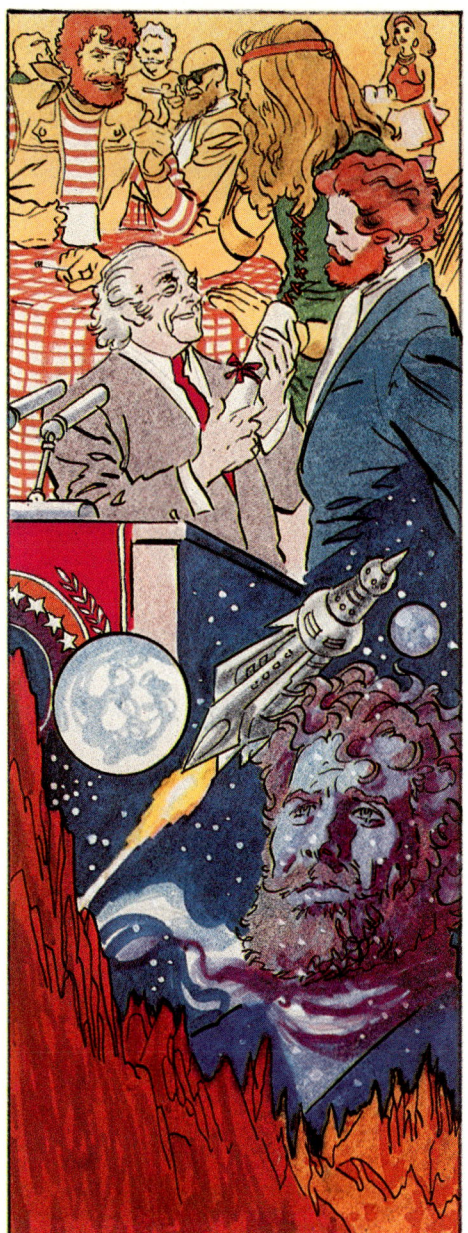

We had had no idea this existed. Greedily, I cast my eyes about. A highly sophisticated system of esthetics lay behind the decor. We would have to revise our entire estimation of Martian culture.

I leaned forward to study a ceremonial table loaded with books.

With my toe, I traced a mosaic on the floor.

"Is your entire city within this one building?"

"Yes, it goes far back into the mountain."

"I see," I said, seeing nothing.

"Shall we begin your friendship with the High Tongue?"

I was trying to photograph the hall with my eyes, knowing I would have to get a camera in here, somehow, sooner or later.

I sat down.

For the next three weeks alphabet-bugs chased each other behind my eyelids whenever I tried to sleep. The sky was an unclouded pool of turquoise that rippled calligraphies whenever I swept my eyes across it.

M'Cwyie tutored me two hours every morning, and occasionally for another two in the evening. I spent an additional fourteen hours a day on my own. At night, the elevator of time dropped me to its bottom floors . . . .

I was six again, learning my Hebrew, Greek, Latin, and Aramaic. I was ten, sneaking peeks at the *Iliad*. **When Daddy wasn't spreading hellfire,** brimstone, and brotherly love, he was teaching me to dig the Word, like in the original.

On the day the boy graduated from high school, with the French, German, Spanish, and Latin awards, Dad Gallinger had told his fourteen-year-old, six-foot scarecrow of a son that he wanted him to enter the ministry. I remember how his son was evasive:

Not telling any **well-meaning parishioners** my new address, I entered into a daily routine of writing poetry and teaching myself Japanese and Hindustani. I grew a fiery beard, drank espresso, and learned to play chess.

After that, it was two years in India with the old Peace Corps—which broke me of my Buddhism, and gave me my *Pipes of Krishna* lyrics and the Pulitzer they deserved.

Then back to the States for my degree, grad work in linguistics, and more prizes.

Then one day a ship went to Mars. The vessel settling in its New Mexico nest of fires contained a new language. —it was fantastic, exotic, and esthetically overpowering. After I had learned all there was to know about it, and written my book, I was famous in new circles:

"Go, Gallinger. Dip your bucket in the well, and bring us a drink of Mars. Go, learn another world —but remain aloof, rail at it gently like Auden— and hand us its soul in iambics."

I came to the land where the sun is a tarnished penny, where the wind is a whip, where two moons play at hot rod games, and a hell of sand gives you the incendiary itches whenever you look at it.

I rose from my twistings on the bunk and crossed the darkened cabin to a port.

I had the High Tongue by the tail already—or the roots, if you want your puns anatomical, as well as correct. The High and Low Tongues were not so dissimilar as they had first seemed. I had enough of the one to get me through the murkier parts of the other. The dictionary I was constructing grew by the day, like a tulip, and would bloom shortly. Every time I played the tapes the stem lengthened.

Now was the time to tax my ingenuity. I had purposely refrained from plunging into the major texts until I could do justice to them. I had been reading minor commentaries, bits of verse, fragments of history—and one thing had impressed me strongly in all that I read.

They wrote about concrete things: rock, sand, water, winds; and the tenor couched within these elemental symbols was fiercely pessimistic. It reminded me of some Buddhist texts, but even more so, I realized from my recent *recherches*, it was like parts of the Old Testament. Specifically, it reminded me of the Book of Ecclesiastes.

That, then, would be it. The sentiment, as well as the vocabulary, was so similar that it would be a perfect exercise. Like putting Poe into French. I would never be a convert to the Way of Malann, but I would show them that an Earthman had once thought the same thoughts, felt similarly.

I switched on my desk lamp.

Vanity of vanities, saith the Preacher, vanity of vanities; all is vanity. What profit hath a man ...

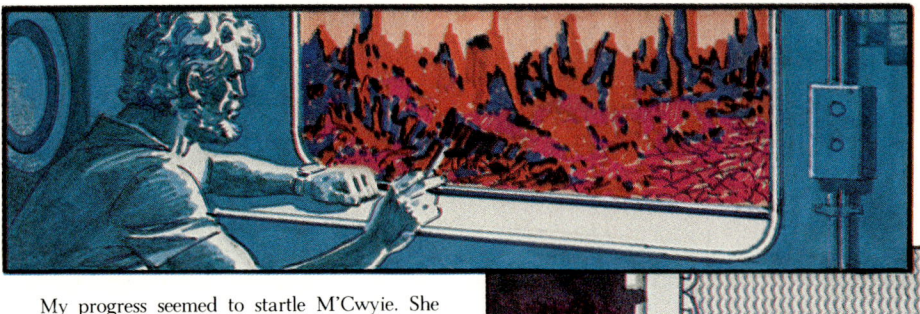

My progress seemed to startle M'Cwyie. She peered at me, like Sartre's Other, across the tabletop. I ran through a chapter in the Book of Locar. I didn't look up, but I could feel the tight net her eyes were working about my head, shoulders, and rabid hands. I turned another page.

They said that life had gotten underway in inorganic matter. They said that movement was its first law, its first law, and that the dance was the only legitimate reply to the inorganic ... the dance's quality its justification,—fication ... and love is a disease in organic matter—Inorganic matter?

I shook my head. I had almost been asleep.

"M'narra."

I stood and stretched. Her eyes outlined me greedily now. So I met them, and they dropped.

"I grow tired. I want to rest awhile. I didn't sleep much last night."

"You wish to relax, and see the explicitness of the doctrine of Locar in its fullness?"

"Pardon me?"

"You wish to see a Dance of Locar?"

"Oh." Their damned circuits of form and periphrasis here ran worse than the Korean! "Yes. Surely. Any time it's going to be done I'd be happy to watch."

"Now is the time. Sit down. Rest. I will call the musicians."

She bustled out through a door I had never been past.

Well, now, the dance was the highest art, according to Locar, not to mention Havelock Ellis, and I was about to see how their centuries-dead philosopher felt it should be conducted.

To the trio who entered with M'Cwyie I must have looked as if I were searching for the marbles I had just lost, bent over like that.

I grinned weakly and straightened up, my face red from more than exertion. I hadn't expected them *that* quickly.

Suddenly I thought of Havelock Ellis again in his area of greatest popularity. The little red-headed doll, wearing, sari-like, a diaphanous piece of the Martian sky, looked up in wonder—as a child at some colorful flag on a high pole.

"Hello," I said, or its equivalent.

"I shall dance," said the red wound in that pale, pale cameo, her face. Eyes, the color of dream and her dress, pulled away from mine.

She drifted to the center of the room.

Standing there, like a figure in an Etruscan frieze, she was either meditating or regarding the design on the floor.

Was the mosaic symbolic of something? I studied it.

The other two were paint-spattered sparrows like M'Cwyie, in their middle years.

M'Cwyie disdained her stool and was seated upon the floor before I realized it. I followed suit.

"What is the dancer's name?"

"Braxa," she replied, without looking at me, and raised her left hand, slowly, which meant yes, and go ahead, and let it begin.

The stringed-thing throbbed like a toothache, and a tick-tocking, like ghosts of all the clocks they had never invented, sprang from the block.

Braxa was a statue, both hands raised to her face, elbows high and outspread.

The music became a metaphor for fire.

Crackle, purr, snap...

She did not move.

The hissing altered to splashes. The cadence slowed. It was water now, the most precious thing in the world, gurgling clear then green over mossy rocks.

Still she did not move.

Glissandos. A pause.

Then, so faint I could hardly be sure at first, the tremble of the winds began. Softly, gently, sighing and halting, uncertain. A pause, a sob, then a repetition of the first statement, only louder.

Were my eyes completely bugged from my reading, or was Braxa actually trembling, all over, head to foot?

She was.

She began a microscopic swaying. A fraction of an inch right, then left. Her fingers opened like the petals of a flower, and I could see that her eyes were closed.

Her eyes opened. They were distant, glassy, looking through me and the walls. Her swaying became more pronounced, merged with the beat.

The wind was sweeping in from the desert now, falling against Tirellian like waves on a dike. Her fingers moved, they were the gusts. Her arms, slow pendulums, descended, began a counter movement.

The gale was coming now. She began an axial movement and her hands caught up with the rest of her body, only now her shoulders commenced to writhe out a figure eight.

The cyclone was twisting around those eyes, its still center. Her head was thrown back, but I knew there was no ceiling between her gaze, passive as Buddha's, and the unchanging skies.

She was a spun weather vane in the air, a clothesline holding one bright garment lashed parallel to the ground. Her shoulder was bare now, and her right breast moved up and down like a moon in the sky, its red nipple appearing momently above a fold and vanishing again.

The music slowed, settled; it had been met, matched, answered. Her garment, as if alive, crept back into the more sedate folds it originally held.

She dropped low, lower, to the floor. Her head fell upon her raised knees. She did not move.

There was silence.

I sought M'Cwyie from the corner of my eye. She raised her right hand.

As if by telepathy the girl shuddered all over and stood. The musicians also rose.

There was a flurry of color and I was alone again with M'Cwyie.

"That is the one hundred-seventeenth of the two thousand, two hundred-twenty-four dances of Locar."

I looked down at her.

"Whether Locar was right or wrong, he worked out a fine reply to the inorganic."

She smiled.

"Are the dances of your world like this?"

"Some of them are similar. I was reminded of them as I watched Braxa —but I've never seen anything exactly like hers."

"She is good," M'Cwyie said. "She knows all the dances."

A hint of her earlier expression which had troubled me... It was gone in an instant.

"I must tend my duties now." She moved to the table and closed the books. "M'narra."

I walked out the door, mounted the jeepster, and roared across the evening into night, my wings of risen desert flapping slowly behind me.

Hours later, after a brief grammar session back home, I heard the voices in the hall. My vent was opened a fraction, so I stood there and eavesdropped:

Morton's fruity treble: "Guess what? He said 'hello' to me awhile ago."

"Regardless of what you think of him, it's going to take me at least a year to learn what he's picked up in three weeks. And I'm just a linguist, not a poet." That was Betty.

Morton must have been nursing a crush on her bovine charms. It's the only reason I can think of for his dropping his guns to say what he did.

"I took a course in modern poetry when I was back at the university," he began. "We read six authors—Yeats, Pound, Eliot, Crane, Stevens, and Gallinger—and on the last day of the semester, when the prof was feeling a little rhetorical, he said, 'These six names are written on the century, and all the gates of criticism and hell shall not prevail against them.'

"Myself," he continued, "I thought his *Pipes of Krishna* and his *Madrigals* were great. I was honored to be chosen for an expedition he was going on, but I think he's spoken two dozen words to me since I met him."

Well bless you, Morton boy. You little pimple-faced, ivy-bred connoisseur! I've never taken a course in my poetry, but I'm glad someone said that. The Gates of Hell. Well now! Maybe I am a missionary, after all!

Only . . . only a missionary needs something to convert people *to*. I have my private system of esthetics, and I suppose it oozes an ethical by-product somewhere. But if I ever had anything to preach, really, even in my poems, I wouldn't care to preach it to such lowlives as you. If you think I'm a slob, I'm also a snob, and there's no room for you in my Heaven—it's a private place, where Swift, Shaw, and Petronius Arbiter come to dinner.

And oh, the feasts we have! The Trimalchio's, the Emory's we dissect!

We finish you with the soup, Morton!

I turned and settled at my desk. I wanted to write something. Ecclesiastes could take a night off. I wanted to write a poem about the one hundred-seventeenth dance of Locar; about a rose following the light, traced by the wind, sick, like Blake's rose, dying . . . . I found a pencil and began. I called it *Braxa*.

In a land of wind and red, where the icy evening of Time freezes milk in the breasts of Life, as two moons overhead—cat and dog in alleyways of dream—scratch and scramble agelessly my flight . . . this final flower turns a burning head.

When I showed my poem to M'Cwyie the next day, she read it through several times, very slowly.

"It is lovely," she said. But what is 'flower'?"

"Oh," I said. "I've never come across your word for 'flower,' but I was actually thinking of an Earth flower, the rose."

"What is it like?"

"Its petals are generally bright red. That's what I meant, on one level, by 'burning heads.' I also wanted it to imply fever, though, and red hair, and the fire of life. The rose, itself, has a thorny stem, green leaves, and a pleasing aroma."

"I wish I could see one."

"I suppose it could be arranged. I'll check."

"Do it, please. You are a—" She used the word for "prophet," or religious poet, like Isaiah or Locar. "—and your poem is inspired. I shall tell Braxa of it."

I declined the nomination, but felt flattered.

This, I decided, was the strategic day, the day on which to ask whether I might bring in the microfilm machine and the camera.

She surprised me by agreeing immediately, but she bowled me over with her invitation.

"Would you like to come and stay here while you do this thing?"

"I should be honored."

"Good. Bring your machines when you want, and I will show you a room."

"Then I will go now and get things ready. Until this afternoon . . ."

I anticipated a little trouble from Emory, but not much. Everyone back at the ship was anxious to see the Martians, poke needles in the Martians, ask them about Martian climate, diseases, politics, and mushrooms—and only four or five had actually gotten to see them. The crew had been spending most of its time excavating dead cities and their acropolises. I figured I would meet with little resistance, and I figured right. In fact, I got the distinct impression that everyone was happy to see me move out.

I stopped in the hydroponics room to speak with our mushroom master, one of my few friends aboard.

"Hi, Kane. Grow any toadstools in the sand yet?"

He sniffed. He always sniffs. Maybe he's allergic to plants.

"Hello, Gallinger. No, I haven't had any success with the toadstools."

"Say, I came down to ask you a favor. I want a rose."

"A what?"

"A rose. You know, a nice red American Beauty job—"

"I don't think it will take in this soil. *Sniff, sniff.*"

"No, you don't understand. I don't want to plant it, I just want the flowers."

"I'd have to use the tanks." He scratched his hairless dome. "It would take at least three months, if you don't mind the wait."

"Not at all. In fact, three months will just make it before we leave." I looked about at the pools of crawling slime. "—I'm moving up to Tirellian today, but I'll be in and out all the time. I'll be here when it blooms."

II

My quarters in the Citadel of Tirellian were directly adjacent to the Temple, so I unpacked and took sixteen 35 mm. shots before starting on the books.

I took stats until I was sick of turning pages without knowing what they said. Then I started translating a work of history.

"In the thirty-seventh year of the Process of Cillen the rains came, which gave rise to rejoicing, for it was a rare and untoward occurrence, and commonly construed a blessing.

"But **what fell** was the blood of the universe, spurting from an artery and the last days were upon us. The final dance was to begin.

"The rains brought the plague that does not kill, and the last passes of Locar began with their drumming . . . ."

I asked myself what the hell Tamur meant, for he was an historian and supposedly committed to fact. This was not their Apocalypse.

Unless they could be one and the same . . . ?

Tirellian's handful of people were the remnant of what had obviously been a highly developed culture. They had had wars, but no holocausts; science, but little technology. A plague, a plague that did not kill . . . ? Could that have done it? How, if it wasn't fatal?

I read on, but the nature of the plague was not discussed. *M'Cwyie! M'Cwyie! When I want to question you most, you are not around!*

I must have been asleep for several hours when Braxa entered my room with a tiny lamp.

"I have come," she said, "to hear the poem."

"What poem?"

"Yours."

I yawned, sat up, and did things people usually do when awakened in the middle of the night to read poetry.

"That is very kind of you, but isn't the hour a trifle awkward?"

"I don't mind," she said.

Someday I am going to write an article for the *Journal of Semantics*, called "Tone of Voice: An Insufficient Vehicle for Irony." I grabbed my robe.

"What sort of animal is that?" she asked, pointing at the silk dragon on my lapel.

"Mythical," I replied. "Now look, it's late. I am tired and M'Cwyie just might get the wrong idea if she learns you were here."

"Wrong idea?"

"You know damned well what I mean!" It was the first time I had had an opportunity to use Martian profanity, and it failed.

"No," she said, "I do not know."

She seemed frightened, like a puppy being scolded without knowing what it has done wrong.

I softened. "Here now, I didn't mean to upset you. On my world there are certain, uh, mores, concerning people of different sex alone together in bedrooms, and not allied by marriage . . . Um, I mean, you see what I mean?"

"No." They were jade, her eyes.

"Well, it's sort of . . . well, it's sex, that's what it is."

A light was switched on in those jade lamps.

"Oh, you mean having children!"

"Yes. That's it! Exactly."

She laughed. It was the first time I had heard laughter in Tirellian. It sounded like a violinist striking his high strings with the bow, in short little chops. When she had finished she moved closer.

"I remember, now," she said. "Half a Process ago, when I was a child, we had such rules. But there is no need for them now."

My mind moved like a tape recorder played at triple speed. Half a Process! No! Yes! Half a Process was two hundred-forty-three years!

—Time enough to learn the 224 dances of Locar.
—Time enough to grow old, if you were human.
—Earth-style human, I mean.

I looked at her again, pale as the white queen in an ivory chess set. She was human, I'd stake my soul—alive, normal, healthy. I'd stake my life—woman, my body . . .

But she was two and a half centuries old, which made M'Cwyie Methuselah's grandma. It flattered me to think of their repeated complimenting of my skills.

But what did she mean "There is no such need for them now?" Why the near-hysteria? Why all those funny looks I'd been getting from M'Cwyie? I knew I was close to something important.

"Tell me," I said, in my Casual Voice, "did it have anything to do with 'the plague that does not kill,' of which Tamur wrote?"

"Yes," she replied, "the children born after the Rains could have no children of their own, and—"

"And what?" I was leaning forward, memory set at "record."

"—and the men had no desire to get any."

I sagged backward against the bedpost. Racial sterility, masculine impotence, following phenomenal weather. Had some vagabond cloud of radioactive junk from God knows where penetrated their weak atmosphere one day? Lone before Shiaparelli saw the canals, mythical as my dragon, before those "canals" had given rise to some correct guesses for all the wrong reasons, had Braxa been alive, dancing, here—damned in the womb since blind Milton had written of another paradise, equally lost?

"Tell me your poem now."

An idea hit me.

"Wait a minute," I said; "I may have something better."

I got up and rummaged through my notebooks, then I returned and sat beside her.

"These are the first three chapters of the Book of Ecclesiastes," I explained. "It is very similar to your own sacred books." I started reading.

I got through eleven verses before she cried out, "Please don't read that! Tell me one of yours!"

I stopped and tossed the notebook onto a nearby table. She was shaking, not as she had quivered that day she danced as the wind, but with the jitter of unshed tears. I put my arm about her shoulders.

"He is so sad," she said, "like all the others."

So I twisted my mind like a bright ribbon, folded it, and tied the crazy Christmas knots I love so well. From German to Martian, with love, I did an impromptu paraphrasal of a poem about a Spanish dancer. I thought it would please her. I was right.

"Ooh," she said again. "Did you write that?"

"No, it's by a better man than I."

"I don't believe you. You wrote it."

"No, a man named Rilke did."

"But you brought it across to my language. Light another match, so I can see how she danced."

I did.

"The fires of forever," she mused, "and she stamped them out, 'with small, firm feet.' I wish I could dance like that."

"You're better than any Gypsy," I laughed, blowing it out.

"No, I'm not. I couldn't do that."

"Do you want me to dance for you?"

"No," I said. "Go to bed."

She smiled, and before I realized it, had unclasped the fold of red at her shoulder.

And everything fell away.

I swallowed, with some difficulty.

"All right," she said.

So I kissed her, as the breath of fallen cloth extinguished the lamp.

III

The days were like Shelley's leaves: yellow, red, brown, whipped in bright gusts by the west wind. Almost all the books were recorded now. It would take scholars years to properly assess their value. Mars was locked in my desk.

Ecclesiastes, abandoned and returned to a dozen times, was almost ready to speak in the High Tongue. I wrote reams of poetry I would have been ashamed of before. Evenings I would walk with Braxa, across the dunes or up into the mountains. Sometimes she would dance for me; she still thought I was Rilke; and I almost kidded myself into believing it. Here I was, staying at the Castle Duino, writing his *Elegies*.

. . . It is strange to inhabit the Earth no more,
to use no longer customs scarce acquired,
nor interpret roses . . .

No! Never interpret roses! Don't. Smell them (sniff, Kane!), pick them, enjoy them. Live in the moment. Hold to it tightly.

The last days were upon us.

A day went by and I did not see Braxa, and a night. And a second. A third.

I was half-mad. I hadn't realized how close we had become, now important she had been. I had fought against questioning roses.

I had to ask. I didn't want to, but I had no choice.

"Where is she, M'Cwyie? Where is Braxa?"

"She is gone," she said.

"I must know."

She looked through me. "She has left us. Up in the hills, I suppose. Or the desert. It does not matter. The dance draws to a close. The Temple will soon be empty."

"I must see her again. We lift off in a matter of days."

"I am sorry, Gallinger."

I stood up.

"I will find her."

I left the Temple. M'Cwyie was a seated statue. My boots were still where I had left them.

All day I roared up and down the dunes, going nowhere. Finally, I had to return for more fuel. Emory came stalking out.

"Okay, make it good. Why the rodeo?"

"Why, I, uh, lost something."

"In the middle of the desert?"

"It's simply that I lost my watch. My mother gave it to me and it's a family heirloom. I want to find it before we leave."

"Hmph!" he snorted. "That's a pretty strange way to look for a watch, riding up and down in a jeepster."

"I could see the light shining off it that way," I offered, lamely.

"Well, it's starting to get dark," he observed. "No sense looking any more today.

"Throw a dust sheet over the jeepster," he directed a mechanic. He patted my arm.

"Come on in and get a shower, and something to eat. You look as if you could use both."

Little fatty flecks beneath pale eyes, thinning hair, and an Irish nose; a voice a decibel louder than anyone else's . . . .

His only qualification for leadership!

The shower was a blessing, clean khakis were the grace of God, and the food smelled like Heaven.

We hacked up our steaks in silence. When we got to the dessert and coffee he said, "They'll be holding a service in the Temple tonight."

"That's right. I'm going to work in my room."

He shrugged his shoulders.

Finally, he said, "Gallinger," and I looked up because my name means trouble. "It shouldn't be any of my business," he said, "but it is. Betty says you have a girl down there."

There was no question mark. It was a statement hanging in the air. Waiting.

Betty, you're a bitch.

"So?" I said, a statement with question mark.

"So," he answered it, "it is my duty, as head of this expedition, to see that relations with the natives are carried on in a friendly, and diplomatic manner."

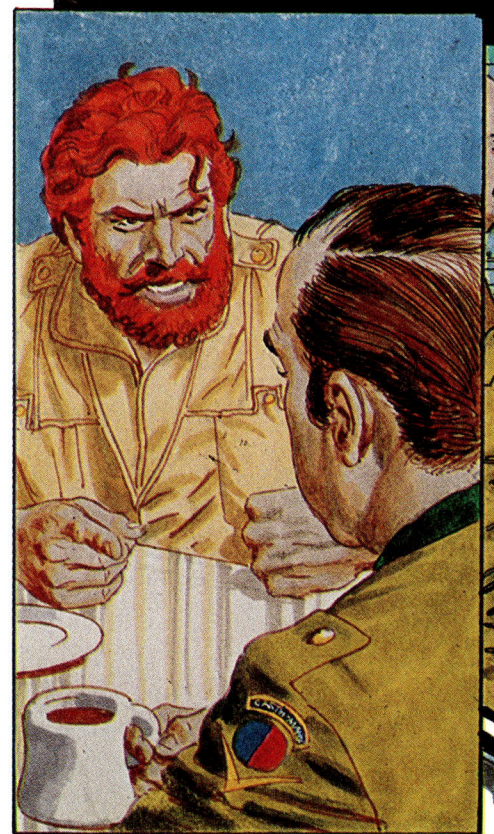

"You speak of them," I said, "as though they are aborigines. Nothing could be further from the truth." I rose. "When my papers are published everyone on Earth will know that truth. I'll tell the tragedy of a doomed race, waiting for death, resigned and disinterested. I'll tell why, and it will break hard, scholarly hearts. I'll write about it, and they will give me more prizes, and this time I won't want them."

"*Do* you have a girl down there?"

"Yes!" I said. Yes, *Claudius! Yes, Daddy! Yes, Emory!* "I do. But I'm going to let you in on a scholarly scoop now. They're sterile. In one more generation there won't be any Martians." I paused, then added, "Except in my papers, except on a few pieces of microfilm and tape. And in some poems, about a girl who did give a damn and could only bitch about the unfairness of it all by dancing."

"Oh," he said.

After awhile: "You *have* been behaving differently these past couple months. You've even been downright civil on occasion. I didn't know anything mattered that strongly to you."

I bowed my head.

"Is she the reason you were racing around the desert?"

I nodded.

"Why?"

I looked up. "Because she's out there, somewhere. I don't know where, or why. And I've got to find her before we go."

He leaned back, opened a drawer, and took out something wrapped in a towel. He unwound it. A framed photo of a woman lay on the table.

"My wife," he said.

It was an attractive face, with big, almond eyes. "I'm a Navy man, you know," he began. "Met her in Japan. She was my wife. When she died I was on the other side of the world. They took my children, and I've never seen them since. I couldn't learn what orphanage, what home, they were put into. That was long ago. Very few people know about it."

"I'm sorry," I said.

"Don't be. Forget it. But"—he shifted in his chair and looked at me—"if you do want to take her back with you—do it. It'll mean my neck, but I'm too old to ever head another expedition like this one. So go ahead."

He gulped his cold coffee.

"Get your jeepster."

I tried to say "thank you" twice, but I couldn't. So I got up and walked out.

"Here it is, Gallinger!" I heard a shout.

I turned on my heel and looked back up the ramp. "Kane!" He was limned in the port, shadow against light, but I had heard him sniff.

I returned the few steps. "Here what is?"

"Your rose."

He produced a plastic container, divided internally. The lower half was filled with liquid. In the other half, was a large, newly opened rose.

"Thank you," I said, tucking it into my jacket.

"Going back to Tirellian, eh?"

"Yes."

"I saw you come aboard, so I got it ready."

"Thanks again."

"It's chemically treated. It will stay in bloom for weeks."

I nodded. I was gone.

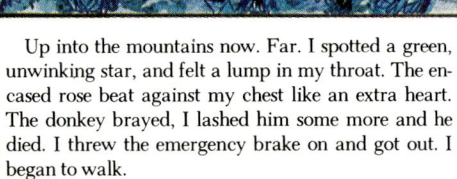

Up into the mountains now. Far. I spotted a green, unwinking star, and felt a lump in my throat. The encased rose beat against my chest like an extra heart. The donkey brayed, I lashed him some more and he died. I threw the emergency brake on and got out. I began to walk.

So cold, so cold it grows. Up here. At night? Why? Why did she do it? Why flee the campfire when night comes on?

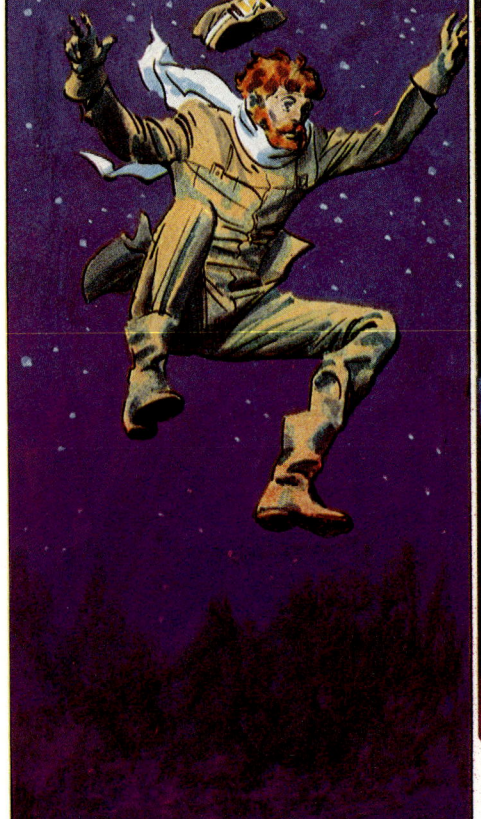

I was up, down, around, and through every chasm, gorge, and pass, with my long-legged strides and an ease of movement never known on Earth. Barely two days remain, my love, and thou hast forsaken me. Why?

I crawled under overhangs. I leaped over ridges. I scraped my knees, an elbow. I heard my jacket tear.

Stones ground underfoot and I dangled over an edge. My fingers so cold. It was hard to grip the rock. I looked down.

Twelve feet or so. I let go and dropped, landed rolling. Then I heard her scream.

I lay there, not moving, looking up. Against the night, above, she called. "Gallinger!"

I lay still.

"Gallinger!" And she was gone.

I heard stones rattle and knew she was coming down some path to the right of me. I jumped up and ducked into the shadow of a boulder.

"Gallinger?"

I stepped out and seized her shoulders.

"Braxa."

She screamed again, then began to cry. It was the first time I had ever heard her cry.

"Why?" I asked. "Why?"

But she only clung to me and sobbed.

Finally, "I thought you had killed yourself."

"Maybe I would have," I said. "Why did you leave Tirellian? And me?"

"Didn't M'Cwyie tell you? Didn't you guess?" She shook all over, then was silent for a long time. I realized suddenly that she was wearing only her flimsy dancer's costume. I pushed her from me, took off my jacket, and put it about her shoulders.

"You'll freeze to death!"

"No," she said, "I won't."

"You really do not know?" she asked.

"No!"

I was transferring the rose-case to my pocket.

"What is that?" she asked.

"A rose," I answered. "You can't make it out much in the dark. I once compared you to one. Remember?"

"Ye-Yes. May I carry it?"

I stuck it in the jacket pocket.

"Well? I'm still waiting for an explanation."

"When the Rains came," she said, "apparently only our men were affected, which was enough . . . Because I—wasn't—affected—apparently—"

"Oh," I said. "Oh." We stood there, and I thought. "Well, why did you run? What's wrong with being pregnant on Mars? Tamur was mistaken. Your people can live again."

She laughed, again that wild violin. I stopped her before it went too far.

"How?" she finally asked, rubbing her cheek.

"Your people live longer than ours. If our child is normal it will mean our races can intermarry. There must still be other fertile women of your race. Why not?"

"You have read the Book of Locar," she said, "and yet you ask me that? Death was decided, voted upon, and passed, shortly after it appeared in this form. But long before, the followers of Locar knew. They decided it long ago. 'We have done all things,' they said, 'we have seen all things, we have heard and felt all things. The dance was good. Now let it end.' "

"You can't believe that."

"What I believe does not matter," she replied. "M'Cwyie and the Mothers have decided we must die. Their very title is now a mockery, but their decisions will be upheld. There is only one prophecy left, and it is mistaken. We will die."

"No," I said.

"What, then?"

"Come back with me, to Earth."

"No."

"All right, then. Come with me now."

"I'm going to talk to the Mothers."

"You can't! There is a Ceremony tonight!"

"But I am going, and you are coming with me, even if I have to carry you—and I'm bigger than you are."

"But you are not bigger than Ontro."

"Who the hell is Ontro?"

"He will stop you, Gallinger. He is the Fist of Malann."

"Go back," he boomed. "Go home to *your* people, Gallinger. Leave *us*!"

If they had refined their martial arts as far as they had their dances, or, worse yet, if their fighting arts were a part of the dance, I was in for trouble.

IV

I scudded the jeepster to a halt in front of the only entrance I knew, M'Cwyie's. Braxa, who had seen the rose in a headlamp, now cradled it in her lap, like our child, and said nothing.

"Are they in the Temple now?" I wanted to know.

The Madonna expression did not change. I repeated the question. She stirred. "Yes," she said, from a distance, "but you cannot go in."

I circled and helped her down.

I led her by the hand, and she moved as if in a trance. In the light of the new-risen moon, her eyes looked as they had the day I met her, when she had danced. I snapped my fingers. Nothing happened.

So I pushed the door open and led her in. The room was half-lighted.

And she screamed for the third time that evening:

"Do not harm him, Ontro! It is Gallinger!"

I had never seen a Martian man before, only women. So I had no way of knowing whether he was a freak, though I suspected it strongly.

I looked up at him.

I had thought I was the tallest man on the planet, but he was seven feet tall and overweight. Now I knew where my giant bed had come from!

"Go back," he said. "She may enter. You may not."

"I must get my books and things."

He raised a huge left arm. I followed it. All my belongings lay neatly stacked in the corner.

"I must go in. I must talk with M'Cwyie and the Mothers."

"You may not."

"The lives of your people depend on it."

"Go on in," I said to Braxa. "Give the rose to M'Cwyie. Tell her that I sent it. Tell her I'll be there shortly."

"I will do as you ask. Remember me on Earth, Gallinger. Good-bye."

"Now will you leave?" he asked. "If you like, I will tell her that we fought and you almost beat me, but I knocked you unconscious and carried you back to your ship."

"No," I said, "either I go around you or go over you, but I am going through."

He dropped into a crouch, arms extended.

"It is a sin to lay hands on a holy man," he rumbled, "but I will stop you, Gallinger."

I looked back six years. I was a student of Oriental Languages at the University of Tokyo. I stood in a thirty-foot circle in the Kodokan, the *judogi* lashed about my high hips by a brown belt. I was *Ik-kyu*, one notch below the lowest degree of expert. I was out of shape, I knew, but I tried hard to force my mind *tsuki no kokoro*.

Somewhere out of the past, a voice said, "*Hajime*, let it begin."

I snapped into my *neko-ashi-dachi* cat-stance, and his eyes burned strangely. He hurried to correct his own position—and I threw it at him!

My one trick!

My long leg lashed up like a broken spring. Seven feet off the ground my foot connected with his jaw as he tried to leap backward.

His head snapped back and he fell. A soft moan escaped his lips. *That's all there is to it*, I thought. *Sorry, old fellow.*

And as I stepped over him, somehow, groggily, he tripped me, and I fell across his body. I couldn't believe he had strength enough to remain conscious after that blow, let alone move. I didn't want to punish him any more.

It was a bar of steel across my windpipe, my carotids. Then I realized that he was still unconscious, and that this was a reflex instilled by countless years of training. I had seen it happen once, in *shiai*.

But it was rare, so very rare!

But he found my throat and slipped a forearm across it before I realized there was a purpose to his action.

No! Don't let it end like this!

I jammed my elbows into his ribs and threw my head back in his face. The grip eased, but not enough. I didn't want to do it, but I reached up and broke his little finger.

The arm went loose and I twisted free.

He lay there panting, face contorted. My heart went out to the fallen giant, defending his people, his religion, following his orders. I cursed myself as I had never cursed before, for walking over him, instead of around.

I couldn't go into the Temple until I got my breath back, until I thought of something to say.

How do you talk a race out of killing itself?

Suddenly—

—Could it happen? Would it work that way? If I read them the Book of Ecclesiastes—if I read them a greater piece of literature than any Locar ever wrote—and as somber—and as pessimistic—and showed them that our race had gone on despite one man's condemning all of life in the highest poetry—showed them that the vanity he had mocked had borne us to the Heavens—would they believe it—would they change their minds?

There was silence all about me.
M'Cwyie had been reading Locar, the rose set at her right hand, target of all eyes.
Until I entered.

Hundreds of people were seated on the floor, barefoot. The few men were as small as the women, I noted.
I had my boots on.

Go all the way, I figured. *You either lose or you win—everything!*
A dozen crones sat in a semicircle behind M'Cwyie. The Mothers.
The barren earth, the dry wombs, the fire-touched.
I moved to the table.
"Dying yourselves, you would condemn your people," I addressed them, "that they may not know the life you have known—the joys, the sorrows, the fullness.—But it is not true that you all must die." I addressed the multitude now. "Those who say this lie. Braxa knows, for she will bear a child—"

They sat there, like rows of Buddhas. M'Cwyie drew back into the semicircle.
"—my child!" I continued, wondering what my father would have thought of this sermon.
". . . And all the women young enough may bear children. It is only your men who are sterile. — and if you permit the doctors of the next expedition to examine you, perhaps even the men may be helped. But if they cannot, you can mate with men of Earth.
"And ours is not an insignificant people, an insignificant place," I went on. "Thousands of years ago, the Locar of our world wrote a book saying that it was. He spoke as Locar did, but we did not lie down, despite plagues, wars, and famines. We did not die. One by one we beat down the diseases, we fed the hungry, we fought the wars, and, recently, have gone a long time without them. We may finally have conquered them. I do not know.

"But we have crossed millions of miles of nothingness. We have visited another world. And our Locar had said, 'Why bother? What is the worth of it? It is all vanity, anyhow.'
"And the secret is," I lowered my voice, as at a poetry reading, "he was right! It *is* vanity! it *is* pride!"
I was working up a sweat. I paused dizzily.
"Here is the Book of Ecclesiastes," I announced, and began:
" 'Vanity of vanities, saith the Preacher, vanity of vanities; all is vanity. What profit hath a man . . .' "
I spotted Braxa in the back, mute, rapt.
I wondered what she was thinking.
And I wound the hours of night about me, like black thread on a spool.

Oh, it was late! I had spoken till day came, and still I spoke. I finished Ecclesiastes and continued Gallinger.
And when I finished there was still only a silence.

The Buddhas, all in a row, had not stirred through the night. And after a long while M'Cwyie raised her right hand. One by one the Mothers did the same.

I knew what that meant. It meant no, do not, cease, and stop. It meant that I had failed. I walked slowly from the room and slumped beside my baggage. Ontro was gone.

After a thousand years M'Cwyie entered.
She said, "Your job is finished."
I did not move.
"The prophecy is fulfilled," she said. "My people are rejoicing. You have won, holy man. Now leave us quickly."
"I'm not a holy man," I said, "just a second-rate poet with a bad case of hubris."
I lit my last cigarette.
Finally, "All right, what prophecy?"
"The Promise of Locar," she replied, as though the explaining were unnecessary, "that a holy man would come from the Heavens to save us in our last hours, if all the dances of Locar were completed. He would defeat the Fist and bring us life."
"How?"
"As with Braxa, and as the example in the Temple."
"Example?"
"You read us his words, as great as Locar's. You read to us how there is 'nothing new under the sun.' And you mocked his words as you read them —showing us a new thing.
"There has never been a flower on Mars," she said, "but we will learn to grow them.
"You are the Sacred Scoffer," she finished. "He-Who-Must-Mock-in-the-Temple—you go shod on holy ground."
"But you voted 'no,' " I said.
"I voted not to carry out our original plan, and to let Braxa's child live instead."

"Oh." The cigarette fell from my fingers. How close it had been! How little I had known!
"And Braxa?"

"She was chosen half a Process ago to do the dances—to wait for you."
"But she said that Ontro would stop me."
M'Cwyie stood there for a long time.

"She had never believed the prophecy herself. Things are not well with her now. She ran away, fearing it was true. When you completed it and we voted, she knew."
"Then she does not love me? Never did?"
"I am sorry, Gallinger. It was the one part of her duty she never managed."
"Duty," I said flatly. . . . Dutydutyduty! Tra-la!
"She has said good-bye; she does not wish to see you again.
". . . and we will never forget your teachings," she added.
"Don't," I said, automatically, suddenly knowing the great paradox which lies at the heart of all miracles. I did not believe a word of my own gospel.
I stood, like a drunken man, and muttered "M'narra."

I went outside, into my last day on Mars.
I left the jeepster there and walked back to the *Aspic*, leaving the burden of life so many footsteps behind me. I went to my cabin, locked the door, and took forty-four sleeping pills.

But when I awakened I was in the dispensary, and alive.
I felt the throb of engines as I slowly stood up and somehow made it to the port.
Blurred Mars hung like a swollen belly above me, until it dissolved, brimmed over, and streamed down my face.

THE THIEF

When Sandor Sandor of Dombeck was four years old he could name all the one hundred forty-nine inhabited worlds in the galaxy. By the time he was ten years old there was no city in the galaxy that anyone could name about which Sandor Sandor did not know *something*. When he took his doctorate in Landography at the age of fourteen, his oral examinations were conducted via closed circuit television. This is because he was afraid to leave his home—and *this* is because on all one hundred forty-nine inhabited worlds in the galaxy there was no remedy for a certain degenerative muscular disease. This disease made it impossible for Sandor to manipulate even the finest prosthetic devices for more than a few minutes without suffering fatigue and great pain; and to go outside he required three such devices—two legs and a right arm—to substitute for those which he had missed out on receiving somewhere along the line before birth.

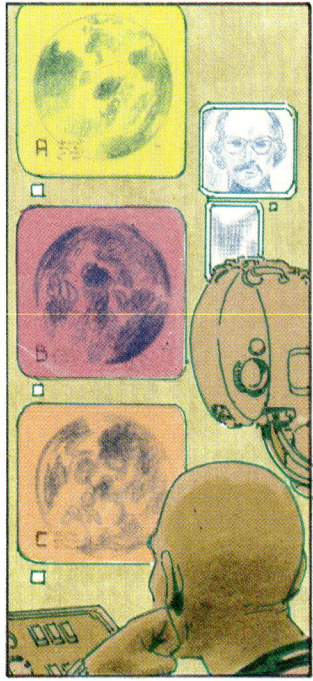

Rather than suffer this pain, or the pain of meeting persons other than his Aunt Faye or his nurse, Miss Barbara, he took his oral examinations via closed circuit television.

It happened that the Interstel Government, which monitors everything, had listened in on Sandor's oral examinations and his defense of his dissertation.

Associate Professor Baines was one of Sandor's very few friends. When the examinations were concluded, Associate Professor Baines stayed on the circuit for several minutes, talking with Sandor. It was during this time that Baines made casual reference to an almost useless (academically, that is) talent of Sandor's.

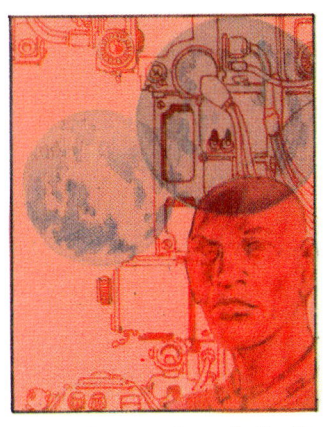

At the mention of it, the government man's ears had pricked forward (he was a Rigellian). He was anxious for a promotion and he recalled an obscure memo....

Associate Professor Baines had mentioned the fact that Sandor Sandor had once studied a series of thirty random photos from all over the civilized galaxy, and that the significant data from these same photos had also been fed into the Department's L-L computer. Sandor had named the correct planet in each case, the land mass in 29, the county or territory in twenty-six, and he had correctly set the location itself within fifty square miles in twenty-three instances. The L-L comp had named the correct planet for twenty-seven.

So it became apparent that Sandor Sandor knew just about every damn street in the galaxy.

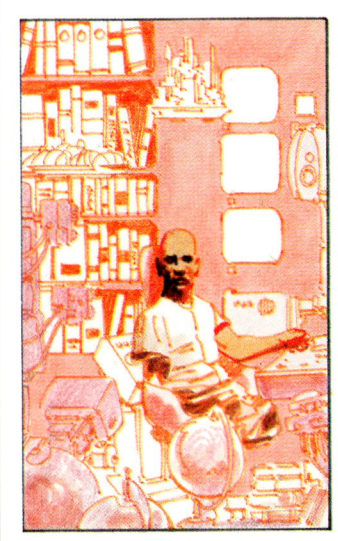

Three years later the Rigellian quit his job, and went to work in private industry, where the promotions were more frequent. *His* memo, and the tape, had been filed, however....

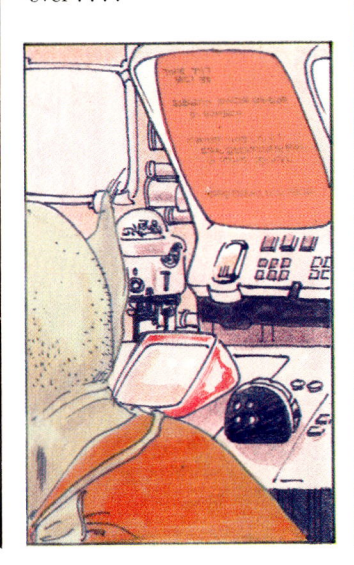

Benedick Benedict was born and grew up on the watery world of Kjum, and his was an infallible power for making enemies of everyone he met.

Gossip was his meat, his drink, and his sex. Shaking hands with him was a mistake, often a catastrophic one. For, as he clung to your hand, pumping it and smiling, his eyes would suddenly grow moist and the tears would dribble down his fat cheeks.

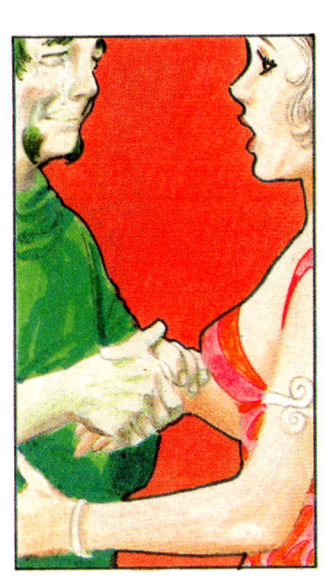

He wasn't sad when this happened. Far from it. It was a somatic conversion from his paranorm reaction.

He was seeing your past life.

He was selective, too; he only saw what he looked for. He saw everything a man wanted to forget, and he talked about it. If you have ever met someone else whom he has also met in this manner, and if this fact shows, he will begin talking of *that* person. Then he will go away and tell others about you.

He was an extremely social animal: he loved attention; he wanted to be admired; he craved audiences.

His abililty extended to inanimate objects as well. Minerals were rare on Kjum, the watery world. If anyone brought him a sample he could hold it and weep and tell them where to dig to hit the main lode. He became wealthy.

From one fish caught in the vast seas of Kjum, he could chart the course of a school of fish.

He did not revel in this either. He simply enjoyed it. For he was one of the nineteen known paranorms in the one hundred forty-nine inhabited worlds in the galaxy, and he knew no other way. Also, he occasionally assisted civil authorities, if he thought their cause just. If he did not, he suddenly lost his power until the need for it vanished. This didn't happen too often though, for an humanitarian was Benedick Benedict, and well-paid, because he was laboratory-tested and clinically-proven. He could pick up thought-patterns originating outside his own skull . . . .

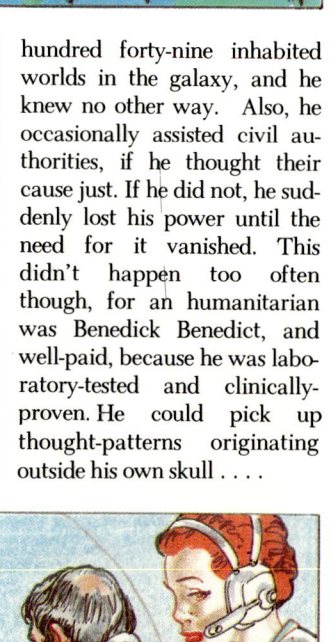

Lynx Links was a man who loved good food and drink, simple clothing, and the company of simple people; he was a man who smiled often and whose voice was soft and melodic.

In his earlier years he had chalked up the most impressive record of any agent ever employed by Interstel Central Intelligence. Forty-eight men and seventeen malicious alien lifeforms had the Lynx dispatched during his fifty-year tenure as a field agent. He was one of the three men in the galaxy to have lived through half a century's employment with ICI. He believed that all life was one and that all men were brothers, and that love rather than hate or fear should rule the affairs of men.

This is the story of how he came to be summoned back from Hosanna, and was joined with Sandor Sandor and Benedick Benedict in the hunt for Victor Corgo, the man without a heart.

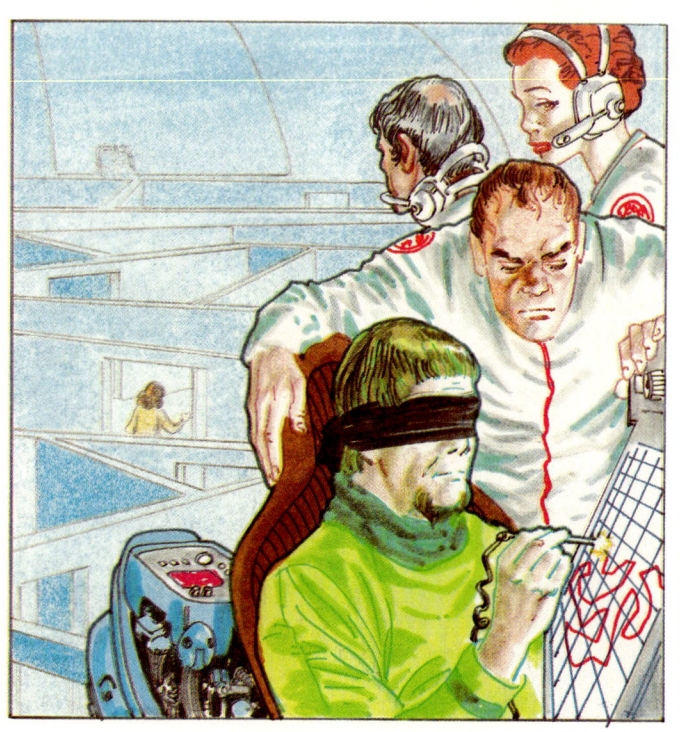

Victor Corgo was captain of the *Wallaby*. Victor Corgo was Head Astrogator, First Mate, and Chief Engineer of the *Wallaby*. Victor Corgo *was* the *Wallaby*. At one time the *Wallaby* was a proud Guardship, meting out the unique justice of the Uniform Galactic Code—in those places where there was no other law.

A terror to brigands, a threat to Codebreakers, and a thorn in the sides of evildoers everywhere, Corgo and his shimmering fungus (which could burn an entire continent under water level within a single day) were the pride of the Guard, the best of the best.

Unfortunately, Corgo sold out. He became a heel .... A traitor. A hero gone bad ...

After forty-five years with the Guard, his pension but half a decade away, he lost his entire crew in an ill-timed raid upon a pirate stronghold on the planet Kilsh, which might have become the hundred-fiftieth inhabited world of Interstel.

Crawling, barely alive, he had made his way half across the great snowfield of Brild, on the main land mass of Kilsh. At the fortuitous moment, death making its traditional noises of approach, he was snatched from out of its traffic lane, so to speak, by the Drillen, a nomadic tribe of intelligent quadrapeds, who took him to their camp and healed his wounds, fed him, and gave him warmth. Later, with the cooperation of the Drillen, he recovered the *Wallaby*.

Crewless, he trained the Drillen. With the Drillen and the *Wallaby* he attacked the pirates.

He won. But he did not stop with that. No.

When he learned that the Drillen had been marked for death under the Uniform Code he sold out his own species. The Drillen had refused relocation to a decent Reservation World. They had elected to continue occupancy of what was to become the hundred-fiftieth inhabited world in Interstel.

Therefore, the destruct-order had been given.

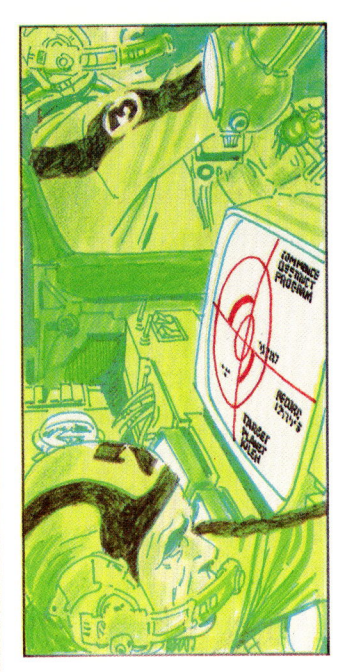

Captain Corgo protested, was declared out of order.

Captain Corgo fought, was beaten, was resurrected, escaped restraint, became an outlaw.

He took the *Wallaby* with him.

As the tractor beams had seized it, as the vibrations penetrated its ebony hull and tore at his flesh, Corgo had called his six Drillen to him, stroked the fur of Mala, his favorite, opened his mouth to speak, and began to die.

"I am sorry ..." he had said.

They gave him a new heart. His old one had fibrillated itself to pieces and could not be repaired. They put the old one in a jar and gave him a shiny, antiseptic egg of throbbing metal, which expanded and contracted at varying intervals, dependent upon what the seed-sized computers they had planted within him told of his breathing and his blood sugar and the output of his various glands.

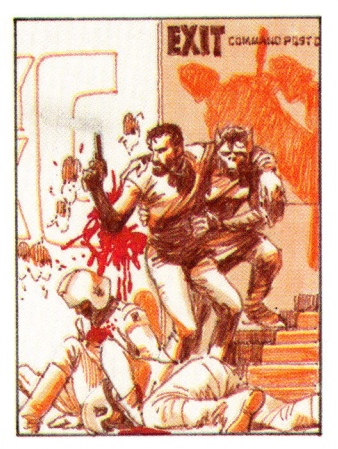

Breaking his parole as an officer, he escaped the Guard Post, taking with him Mala, the only remaining Drillen in the galaxy. Her five fellows had not survived scientific inquiry as to the nature of their internal structures. The rest of the race, of course, had refused relocation.

Then did the man without a heart make war upon mankind.

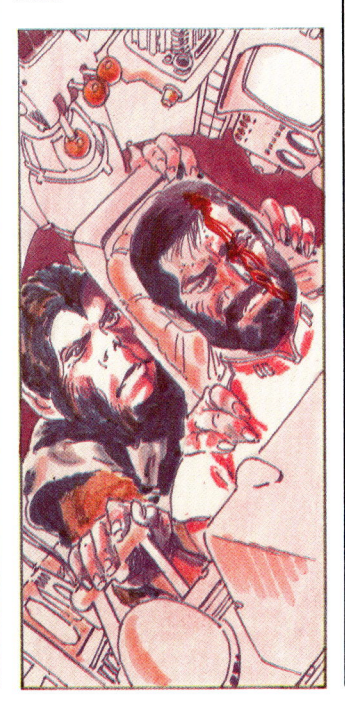

The day they came together on Dombeck, Benedick held forth his hand, smiled, said: "Mister Sandor . . ."

As his hand was shaken, his smile reversed itself. Then it went away from his face. He was shaking an artificial hand.

Sandor nodded, dropped his eyes.

Benedick turned to the big man with the eyepatch.

". . . and you are the Lynx?"

"That is correct, my brother. You must excuse me if I do not shake hands. It is against my religion. I believe that life does not require reassurance as to its oneness."

"Of course," said Benedick. "Let us talk of this man Corgo."

"The ICI man told me that insurance associations have lodged protests with their Interstel representatives."—the Lynx.

"Yes"—Sandor, biting his lip. "Do you gentlemen mind if I remove my legs?"

"Please do," said Benedick.

Sandor leaned forward.

"Were you in an accident?" asked Benedick.

"Birth"—Sandor.

The Lynx raised a decanter of brownish liquid to the light. He stared through it.

"It is a local brandy"—Sandor. "Quite good. Somewhat like the *xmili* of Bandla, only nonaddictive. Have some."

The Lynx did, keeping it in front of him all that evening.

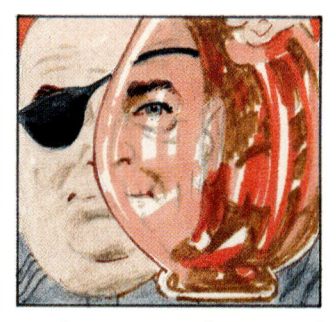

"Corgo is a destroyer of property," said Benedick.

Sandor nodded.

". . . and a defrauder of insurance associations, a defacer of planetary bodies, a deserter from the Guard—"

"A murderer"—Sandor.

". . . and a zoophilist," finished Benedick.

"Aye"—the Lynx, smacking his lips.

"So great an offender against public tranquility is he that he must be found."

"Yes, we must locate him and kill him," said Benedick.

"The two pieces of equipment . . . Are they present?"—the Lynx.

"Yes, the phase-wave is in the next room. The other item is in the bottom drawer of this desk."

"Then why do we not begin now?"

"Very well," answered Sandor, "one of you will have to open the drawer. It is in the brown-glass jar, to the back."

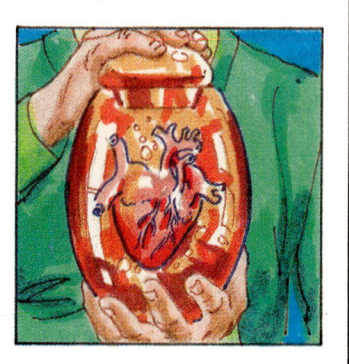

A great sob escaped him after a time, as he sat there with rows of worlds at his back, tears on his cheeks, and Corgo's heart clutched in his hands.

It is cold and dim. . . ."

"Where?"—the Lynx.

"It is a small place. A room? Cabin? Instrument panels . . . A humming sound . . . Vibration . . . Hurt!"

"What is he doing?"—Sandor.

". . . Sitting, half-lying—Furry one at his side, sleeping. Twisted—angles—everything—Hurt!"

"The *Wallaby*, in transit"—Lynx.

"Where is he going?"—Sandor.

"HURT!" shouted Benedick.

Sandor dropped the heart into his lap.

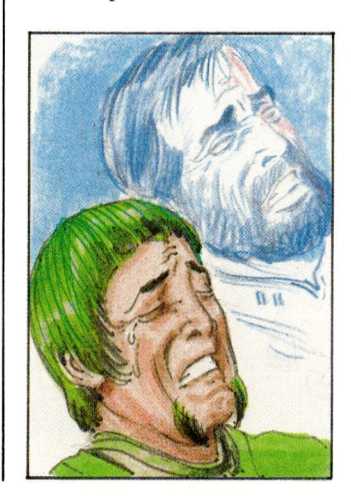

"The *Wallaby* was fast-phasing somewhere, and Corgo was in phase-sleep. It is a disturbing sensation to fast-phase while fully conscious. You found him at a bad time—while under sedation and subject to continuum-impact. Perhaps tomorrow will be better...."

"I hope so."

"Yes, tomorrow"—Sandor.

"Tomorrow . . . Yes.

"There *was* one other thing," he added.

"A burn-job?"—Lynx.

"Yes. He is on his way to do it."

The Lynx stood.

"I will phase-wave ICI and advise them. They can check which worlds are presently being mined. Have you any ideas how soon?"

"No, I can not tell that."

"I'll call in now—and we'll try again . . . ."

Mala whimpered and moved nearer her Corgo, for she was dreaming an evil dream: They were back on the great snowfield of Brild, and she was trying to help him. He kept slipping though, rising more slowly each time and moving ahead at an even slower pace. He tried to kindle a fire, but the snow-devils spun and toppled like icicles falling from the seven moons, and the dancing green flames died as soon as they were born.

Finally, on the top of a mountain of ice she saw them.

There were three . . . springing over drifts and ridges of ice, their arms extended before them.

Silent they came, pausing only as the one sniffed the air, the ground . . . . She could hear their breathing now, feel their heat . . . . In a matter of moments they would arrive . . . .

Mala whimpered and moved nearer her Corgo.

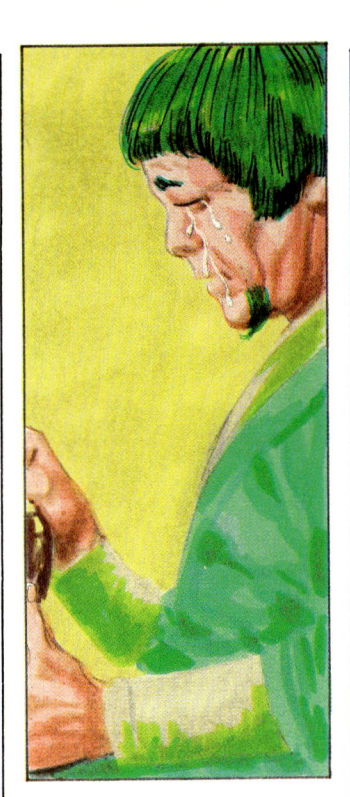

For three days Benedick tried, clutching Corgo's heart like a gypsy's crystal, watering it with his tears. His head ached for hours after, each time that he met the continuum-impact. He wept long, moist tears for hours beyond contact, which was unusual. He had always withdrawn from immediate pain before. He hurt each time that he touched Corgo and he touched Corgo eleven times during those three days, and then his power went away, really.

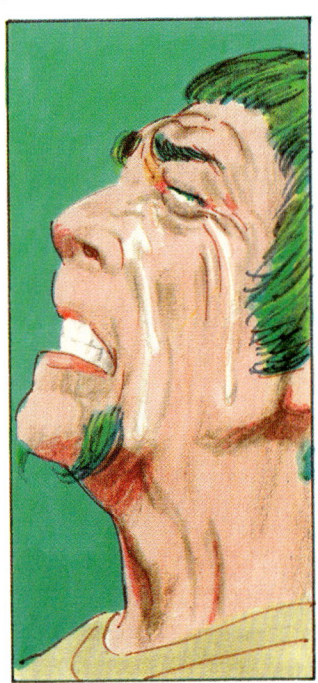

Seated, like a lump of dark metal on the hull of the *Wallaby*, he stared across six hundred miles at the blazing hearth which he had stoked to steel-tempering heights; and he *felt* like a piece of metal, resting there upon an anvil, waiting for the hammer to fall again, as it always did, waiting for it to strike him again and again, and to beat him to a new toughness. Sweating as he watched, smiling, Corgo took pictures.

When one of the nineteen known paranorms in the one hundred forty-nine inhabited worlds in the galaxy suddenly loses his powers, and loses them at a crucial moment, it is like unto the old tales wherein a princess is stricken one day with an unknown malady and the king, her father, summons all his wise men and calls for the best physicians in the realm.

In the end, the matter was settled neatly by Sandor's nurse Miss Barbara, who happened onto the veranda one afternoon as Benedick sat there fanning himself and drinking *xmili*.

"Why Mister Benedict!" she announced, "fancy meeting you out here! I thought you were in the library with the boys."

"As you can see, I am not," he said, staring at his knees.

"Well, it's nice just to pass the time of day sometimes, too. To rest from the hunting of Victor Corgo . . ."

"Please, you're not supposed to know about the project. It's top secret and critical—"

"Dear Sandor talks in his sleep every night—so much. You see, I tuck him in each evening and sit there until he drifts away to dreamland, poor child."

"Mm, yes. Please don't talk about the project, though."

"Why? Isn't it going well?"

"No!"

"Why not?"

"Because of *me*, if you must know! I've got a block of some kind. The power doesn't come when I call it."

"Oh, how distressing! You mean you can't peep into other persons' minds any more?"

"Exactly."

"Dear me. Well, let's talk about something else then. Did I ever tell you about the days when I was the highest-paid courtesan on Sordido V?"

Benedick's head turned slowly in her direction.

"Nooo . . ." he said. "You mean *the* Sordido?"

"Oh yes. Bright Bad Barby, the Bouncing Baby, they used to call me. They still sing ballads, you know."

"Yes, I've heard them. Many verses . . . ."

Later that afternoon, the Lynx wandered out into the veranda during the course of his meditations. He saw there Miss Barbara, with Benedick seated beside her, weeping.

"What troubles thy tranquility, my brother? he inquired.

"Nothing! Nothing at all! It is wonderful and beautiful, everything! My power has come back—I can feel it!" He wiped his eyes on his sleeve.

"Bless thee, little lady!" said the Lynx, seizing Miss Barbara's hand. "Thy simple counsels have done more to heal my brother than have all these highly-paid medical practitioners brought here at great expense."

"Come brother, let us away to our task again!"

"Yes, let us!—Oh thank you, Bright Barby!"

"Don't mention it."

Benedick's eyes clouded immediately, as he took the tattered blood-pump into his hands. He leaned back, stroking it, and moist spots formed on either side of his nose, grew like well-fed amoebas, underwent mitosis, and dashed off to explore in the vicinity of his shelf-like upper lip.

He sighed once, deeply.
"Yes, I am there."
He blinked, licked his lips.
". . . It is night. Late. It is a primitive dwelling. Mud-like stucco, bits of straw in it . . . All lights out, but for the one from the machine, and its spillage—"

"Machine?"—Lynx.
"What machine?"—Sandor.
". . . Projector. Pictures on wall . . . World—big, filling whole picture-field—patches of fire on the world, up near the top. Three places—"

"Bhave VII!"—Lynx. "Six days ago!

"Shoreline to the right goes like this . . . And to the left, like this . . . ."

His right index finger traced patterns in the air.

"Bhave VII"—Sandor.

"Happy and not happy at the same time—hard to separate the two. Guilt, though, is there—but pleasure with it. Revenge . . . . The dog is lying on our foot. The foot is asleep, but we do not want to disturb the dog, for it is Mala's favorite thing—her only toy, companion, living doll, four-footed . . . . Light leaks down upon them . . . . The breeze is warm. Insects buzz by the projector—pterodactyl silhouettes on the burning world—"

"Can you see what is beyond the window?"—Sandor.

". . . Outside are trees—short ones—just outlines, squat. Can't tell where trunks begin . . . Foliage too thick, too close. Too dark .out.—Off in the distance a tiny moon . . . Something like *this* on a hill . . ." His hands shaped a turnip impaled on an obelisk. "Not sure how far off, how large, what color, or what made of . . ."

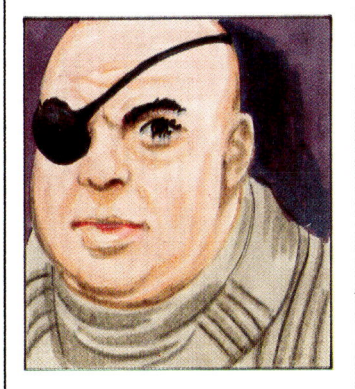

"Is the name of the place in Corgo's mind?"—Lynx.

"If I could touch him, with my hand, I would know it. Only receive impressions *this* way, though—surface thoughts. He is not thinking of where he is now.... An insect lights on Dilk's nose. She brushes it away. Segmented, two sets of wings, about five millimeters in length..."

"How many entrances are there to the place?"—Lynx.

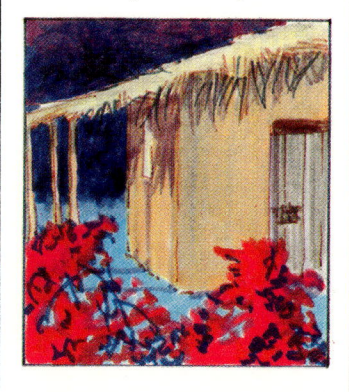

"Two. One doorway at each end of the hut."

"Anything else?"

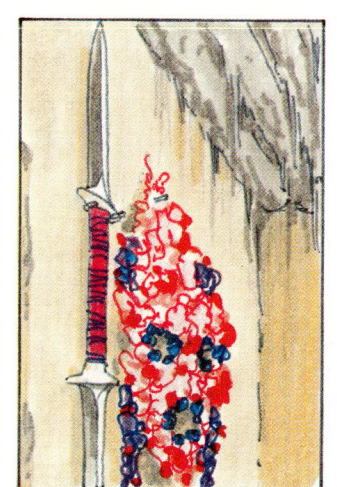

"On the wall a sword—long hilt, very long, two-handed—short blades, though... Beside it, a mask of—flowers? The blades shine; the mask is dull. Looks like flowers, though. Many little ones.... Mala is restless. She nuzzles our shoulder now. We rub our chin. Need a shave... The hell with it! We're not standing any inspections! Drink—one, two—all gone!"

Sandor had threaded a tape into his viewer, and he was spinning it and stopping it. He checked his worlds chronometer.

"Outside," he asked, "does the moon seem to be moving up, or down, or across the sky?"

"Across. Right to left. It seems about a quarter past zenith."

"Any coloration to it?"

"Orange, with three black lines. One starts at about eleven o'clock, crosses a quarter of its surface, drops straight down, cuts back at seven."

"Any constellations you can make out?"—Lynx.

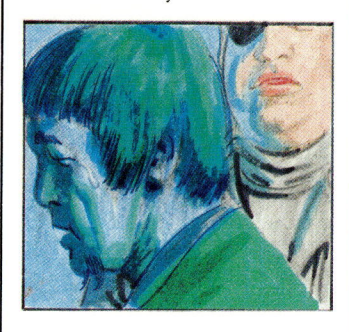

"... Head isn't turned that way now, wasn't turned toward the window long enough. Now there is a noise, far off ..."

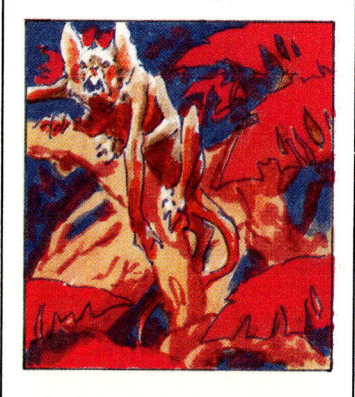

A high-pitched chattering, almost metallic. Animal. He sees a six-legged tree creature, half the size of a man, reddish-brown hair, sparse."

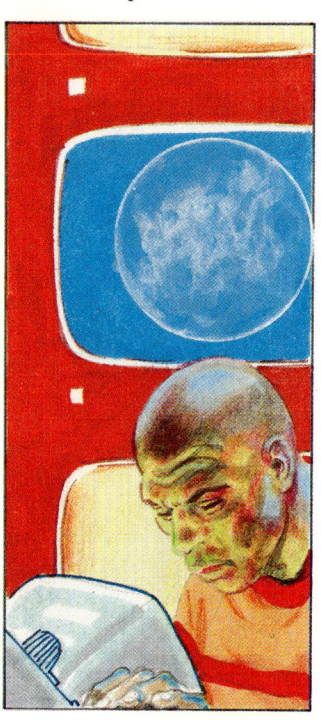

"He is on Disten, the fifth world of Blake's System," said Sandor. "Night-side means he is on the continent Didenlan. The moon Babry, well past zenith now, means he is to the east. A Mellar-mosque indicates a Mella-Muslim settlement. The blade and the mask seem Hortanian. I am sure they were brought from further inland. It is on the Dista River, north bank. There is much jungle about—and it is least settled to the northwest, because of the hills, rocks, and—"

"That's where he is then!"—Lynx. "Now here is how we'll do it. He has, of course, been sentenced to death. I believe—yes, I know!—there is an ICI Field Office on the second world—whatever its name—of that System."

"Nirer"—Sandor.

"Yes. Hmm, let's see... Two agents will be empowered as executioners. They will land their ship to the northwest of Landear, enter the city, and find where the man with the strange four-legged pet settled, the one who arrived within the past six days. Then one agent will enter the hut and ascertain whether Corgo is within. He will retreat immediately if Corgo is present, signaling to the other who will be hidden behind those trees or whatever. The second man will then fire a round of fragmentation plaster through the unguarded window. Each will carry a two-hundred channel laser sub-gun with vibrating head. I'll phase-wase it to Central now.

He hurried from the room.
Benedick, still holding the thing, his shirt-front soaking, continued:
" 'Fear not, my lady dark. He is but a puppy, and he howls at the moon . . . .' "

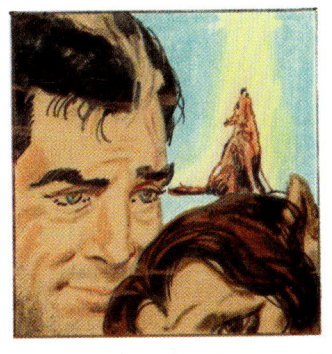

It was thirty-one hours and twenty minutes later when the Lynx received and decoded the two terse statements:

EXECUTIONERS THE WAY OF ALL FLESH.
THE WALLABY HAS JUMPED AGAIN.

He licked his lips. His comrades were waiting for the report, and *they* had succeeded—they had done their part, had performed efficiently and well. It was the Lynx who had missed.

"We begin again," he told them.

Benedick's powers—if anything, stronger than ever—survived continuum-impact seven more times. Then he described a new world: Big it was, and many-peopled—bright—dazzling, under a blue-white sun; yellow brick brick everywhere, neo-Denebian architecture, greenglass windows, a purple sea nearby . . . .

No trick at all for Sandor: "Phillip's World," he named it, then told them the city: "Delles."

"This time *we* burn *him*," said the Lynx, and he was gone from the room.

"I'm not preconning," said Benedick, "but I'll give you odds, like three to one—on Corgo's escaping again."

"Why?"

"When he abandoned humanity he became something less, and more. He is not ready to die."

"What do you mean?"

"I hold his heart. He gave it up, in all ways. But he will reclaim it one day. Then he will die."

"How do you know?"

". . . A feeling."

"How do you know?"

". . . A feeling. I *know* people, have known many. I do not pretend to know all about them. But weakness—yes, about those I know much.

He was troubled. How had they found him so quickly? He had had close brushes with them before—many of them, over the years. But he was cautious, and he could not see where he had failed this time, could not understand how Interstel had located him. Even his last employer did not know his whereabouts.

He shook his head and phased for Phillip's world.

He took elaborate pains, in-phasing and out-phasing in random directions; he gave Mala a golden collar with a two-way radio in its clasp, wore its mate within his death-ring; he converted much currency, left the *Wallaby* in the care of a reputable smuggler and crossed Phillip's World to Delles-by-the-Sea. He was fond of sailing, and he liked the purple waters of this planet. He rented a large villa near the Delles Dives—slums to the one side, Riviera to the other. This pleased him. He still had dreams; he was not dead yet.

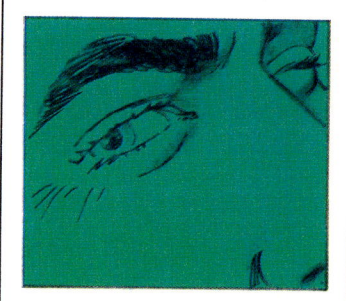

Sleeping, perhaps, he had heard a sound. Then he was suddenly seated on the side of his bed. "Mala?"

She was gone. The sound he'd heard had been the closing of a door. He activated the radio. "What is it?" he demanded.

"I have the feeling we are watched again," she replied, through her ring. ". . . Only a feeling, though." Her voice was distant, tiny.

"Why did you not tell *me*? Come back—now."

"No. I match the night and can move without sound. I will investigate."

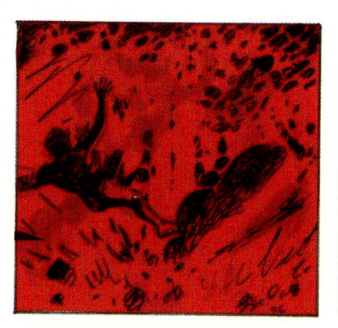

They were above him. This time they had been cautioned not to close with him, but to strike from a distance.

Something struck him in the head and the shoulder. He fell, turning. He was struck in the chest, the stomach.

Then there was another burst.

Blackness followed.

They thought they had succeeded.

"Nothing," Benedick had said, smiling through his tears.

So that day they celebrated, and the next.

But Corgo's body had not been recovered.

Almost half a block had been hurled down, though, and eleven other residents could not be located either. ICI, however, requested that the trio remain together on Dombeck for another ten days, while further investigations were carried out.

Benedick laughed.

"Nothing," he repeated. "Nothing."

But there is a funny thing about a man without a heart: His body does not live by the same rules as those of others: No. The egg in his chest is smarter than a mere heart, and it is the center of a wonderful communications system. Dead itself, it has resources which a living heart does not command.

As the burns and lacerations were flashed upon the screen of the body, it moved itself to an emergency level of function; the glands responded and poured forth their juices; muscles were activated as if by electricity.

Corgo was only half-aware of the inhuman speed with which he moved through the storm of heat and the hail of building materials. It tore at him, but this pain was canceled. The egg took stock of the cost of the action. Down, down did it send him. Into the depths of subcoma. Standard-model humans cannot decide one day that they wish to hibernate, lie down, do it. But Corgo had a built-in survival kit with a mind of its own. So it did the things a heart cannot do, while maintaining its own functions.

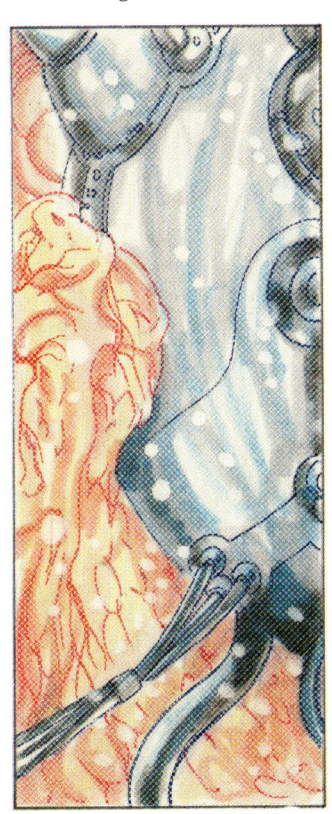

It hurled him into the blackness of sleep without dreams, of total unawareness. For only at the border of death itself could his life be retained, be strengthened, grow again. To approach this near the realm of death, its semblance was necessary.

Therefore, Corgo lay dead in the gutter.

People, of course, flock to the scene of any disaster.

Those from the Riviera pause to dress in their best catastrophe clothing. Those from the slums do not, because their wardrobes are not as extensive.

There was an explosion, but it was seconds before he realized it. Then he saw the flames. He looked up, saw the hoverglobe. A memory appeared within his mind and he winced and continued to watch. He was loaded with zimlak; things were fuzzy.

After a time he saw the man, moving at a fantastic pace across the landscape of hell. The man fell in the street. There was more burning, and then the globe departed.

The impressions finally registered, and his disaster-reflex made him approach.

"... Captain," he said, as he stared into the angular face with the closed dark eyes. "Captain . . ."

He covered his own face with his hands and they came away wet. "On the deck my Captain lies . . . cold . . . dead." His sob was a jagged thing, until he was seized with a spell of hiccups. Then he steadied his hands and raised an eyelid.

Corgo's head jerked two inches to his left, away from the brightness of the flames.

The man laughed in relief.

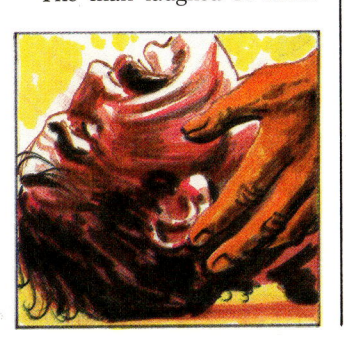

"You're alive, Cap! You're still alive!"

The thing that was Corgo did not reply.

" 'Do not move the victim'— that's what it says in the Manual. But you're coming with me, Cap. I remember now . . . . It was after I left. But I remember . . . —Wish I wasn't so fogged . . . I'm sorry, Cap. You were always good, to the men, good to me. Ran a tight ship, but you were good . . . Old *Wallaby*, happy . . . Yes. We'll go now. Fast as we can. Before the Morbs come.—Yes. I remember . . . you. Good man, Cap. Yes."

So, the *Wallaby* had made its last jump, according to the ICI investigation which followed. But Corgo still dwelled on the dreamless border.

After the ten days had passed, the Lynx and Benedick still remained with Sandor. Sandor was not anxious for them to go. He had never been employed before; he liked the feeling of having co-workers about, persons who shared memories of things done. Benedick was loathe to leave Miss Barbara, one of the few persons he could talk to and have answer him, willingly. The Lynx liked the food and the climate. So they stayed on.

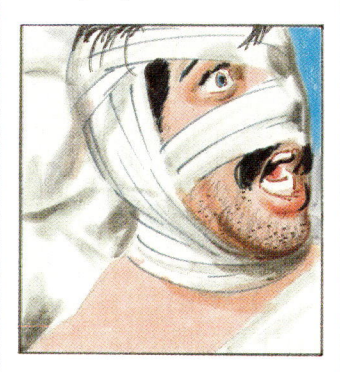

Returning from death is a deadly slow business. Reality does the dance of the veils, and it is a long while before you know what lies beneath them all (if you ever really do).

When Corgo had formed a rough idea, he cried out:

"Mala!"

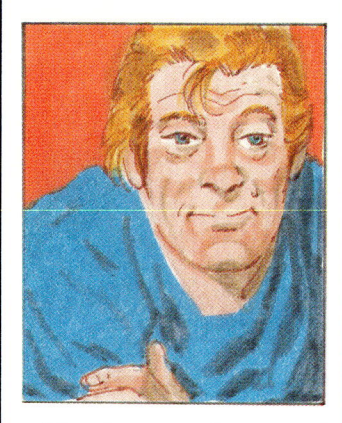

Then he saw a face out of times gone by.

"Sergeant Emil . . . ?"

"Yes, sir. Right here, Captain."

"Where am I?"

"My hutch, sir. Yours got burnt out."

"What of my—pet? A Drillen . . ."

"There was only you I found, sir—no one, nothing, else. Uh, it was almost a month-cycle ago that it happened . . . ."

"I wonder how they found me, so fast—again . . . ?"

"I don't know, sir. Would you like to try some broth now?"

"Later."

He lay back and wondered.

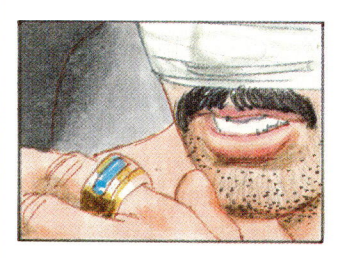

There was her voice. He had been dozing all day and he was part of a dream. "Corgo, are you there? Are you there, Corgo? Are you . . ." His hand! The ring. "Mala! Where are you?"

"In a cave, by the sea. Everyday I have called to you. Are you alive?"

"I am alive. How have you kept yourself?"

"I go out at night. Steal food from the large dwellings with the green windows like doors—for Dilk and myself."

"The puppy? Alive, too?"

"Yes. He was penned in the yard on that night . . . . Where are you?"

"Wait until dark, I'll get you directions.—No. I'll send him after you, my friend . . . . Where is your cave?"

In the days that followed, his strength returned to him. He played chess with Emil and talked with him of their days together in the Guard. He laughed, for the first time in many years.

Mala kept to herself, and to Dilk. Occasionally, Corgo would feel her eyes upon him.

But whenever he turned, she was always looking in another direction. He realized that she had never seen him being friendly with anyone before. She seemed puzzled.

He drank *zimlak* with Emil, they ventured off-key ballads together . . . .

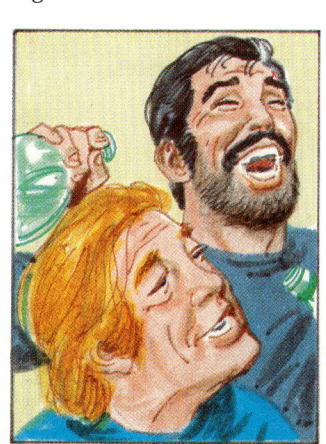

Then one day it struck him.

"Emil, there is a price on my head—you know?"

"I know."

"A pretty large reward. It's yours, by right."

"I couldn't turn you in, sir."

"Nevertheless, the reward is yours. Twice over. I'll send you that amount—a few weeks after I leave here."

"I couldn't take it, sir."

"Why not?"

"Nothing, exactly . . . I just don't want any of it. I'll take this you gave me for the food and stuff. But no more, that's all."

"Oh . . . All right, Emil. Any way you like it. Another game now? I'll spot you a bishop and three pawns this time."

"Very good, sir."

"We had some good time together, eh? Cygnus VII—the purple world with the Rainbow Women?"

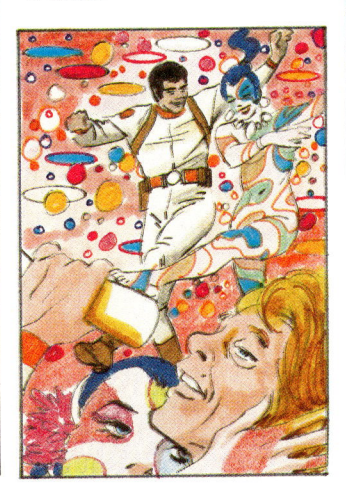

"Took me three weeks to get that dye off me. Thought at first it was a new disease. Flames! I'd love to ship out again!"

Corgo paused in mid-move.

"Hmm . . . You know, Emil . . . It might be that you could."

"What do you mean?"

Corgo finished his move.

"Aboard the *Wallaby*. It's here, in Unassociated Territory, waiting for me.

Emil replaced the knight he had raised, looked up, looked back down. "I—I don't know what to say, Cap. I never thought you'd offer me a berth . . ."

"Why not? I could use a good man. Lots of action, like the old days. Plenty cash. No cares. We want three months' leave on Tau Ceti and we write our own bloody orders. We take it!"

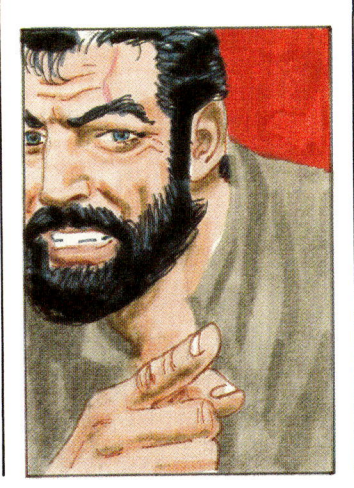

"I don't know how to say it, Cap . . . . But when we—burnt places, before—well, it was criminals—pirates, Codebreakers—you know. Now . . . Well, now I hear you burn—just people. Uh, non-Codebreakers. Like, just plain civilians. Well—I could not."

Corgo did not answer. Emil moved his knight.

"I hate them, Emil," he said, after a time. "Every lovin' one of them, I hate them. Do you know what they did on Brild? To the Drillen?"

"Yessir. But it wasn't civilians, and not the miners. It was not *everybody*. It wasn't every lovin' one of them, sir.—I just couldn't."

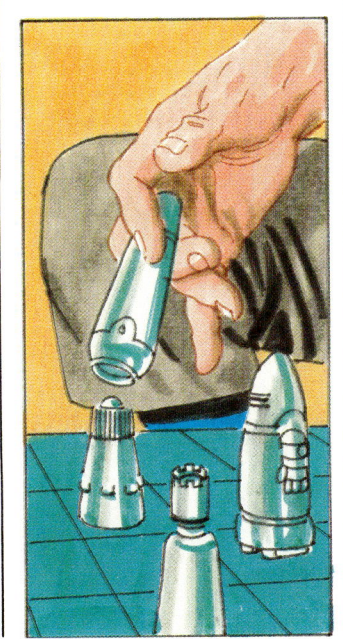

"That's why my money is no good with you?"

"No, sir. That's not it, sir. Well maybe part . . . But only part. I just couldn't take pay for helping someone I—respected, admired."

"You use the past tense."

"Yessir. But I still think you got a raw deal, and what they did to the Drillen was wrong and bad and—evil—but you can't hate everybody for that, sir, because *everybody* didn't do it."

"They countenanced it, Emil —which is just as bad. I am able to hate them all for that alone. And people are all alike, all the same. I burn without discrimination these days, because it doesn't really matter *who*. The guilt is equally distributed. Mankind is commonly culpable."

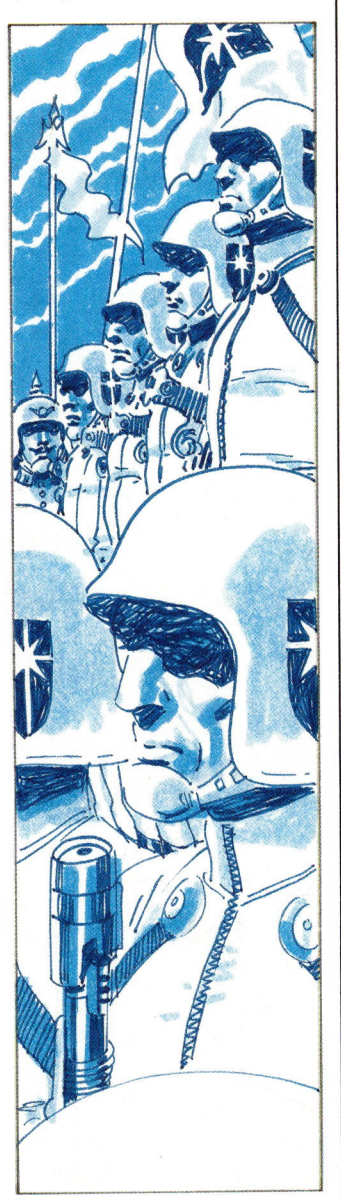

"No, sir, begging your pardon, sir, but in a system as big as Interstel not everybody knows what everybody else is up to. There are those feeling the same way you do, and there are those as don't give a damn, and those who just don't know a lot of what's going on, but who would do something about it if they knew, soon enough."

"It's your move, Emil."

After a couple of moves:

"You know, if I were to give it up—the burning, I mean—and just do some ordinary, decent smuggling with the *Wallaby*, it would be okay. With me. Now. I'm tired. I'm so damned tired I'd just like to sleep—oh, four, five, six years, I think. Supposing I stopped the burning and just shipped stuff here and there—would you sign on with me then?"

"I'd have to think about it, Cap."

"Do that, then. Please. I'd like to have you along."

"Yessir. Your move, sir."

It would not have happened that he'd have been found by his actions, because he *did* stop the burning; it would not have happened—because he was dead on ICI's books—that anyone would have been looking for him. It happened, though—because of a surfeit of *xmili* and good will on the part of the hunters.

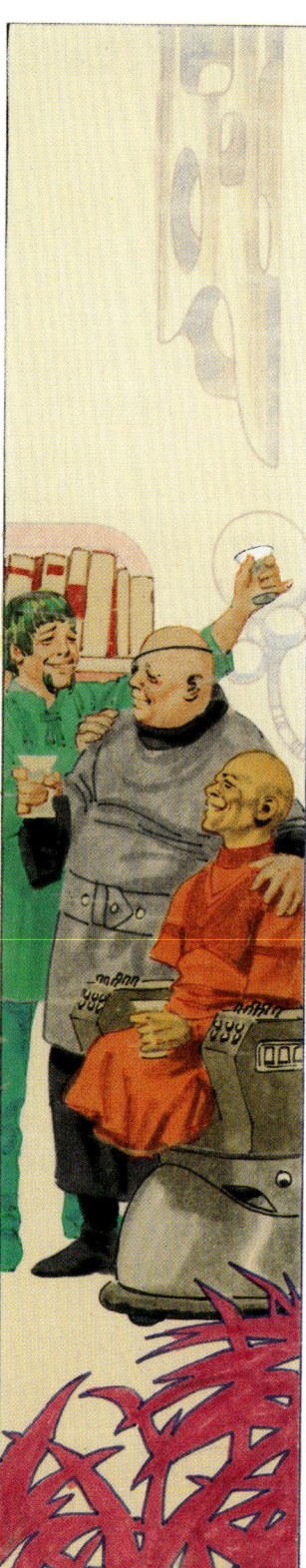

On the eve of the breaking of the fellowship, nostalgia followed high spirits. So, in the library, drinking, and eating and talking, they returned to the hunt. Dead tigers are always the best kind.

Of course, it wasn't long before Benedick picked up the heart, and held it as a connoisseur would an art object—gently, and with a certain mingling of awe and affection.

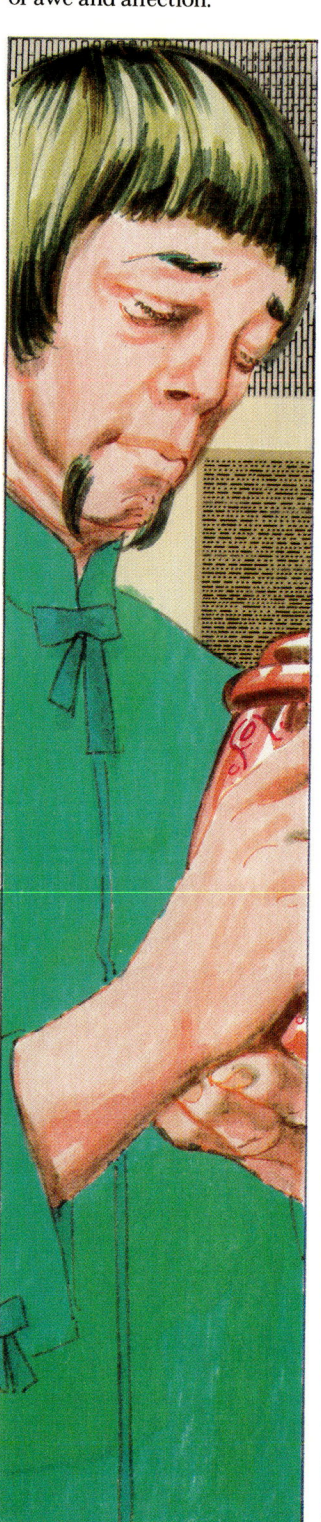

As they sat there, an odd sensation crept into the pudgy paranorm's stomach and rose slowly, like gas, until his eyes burned.

"I—I'm reading," he said.

"Of course"—the Lynx.

"Yes"—Sandor.

"Really!"

"Naturally"—the Lynx. "He is on Disten, fifth world of Blake's System, in a native hut outside Landear—"

"No"—Sandor. "He is on Phillip's World, in Delles-by-the-Sea."

They laughed, the Lynx a deep rumble, Sandor a gasping chuckle.

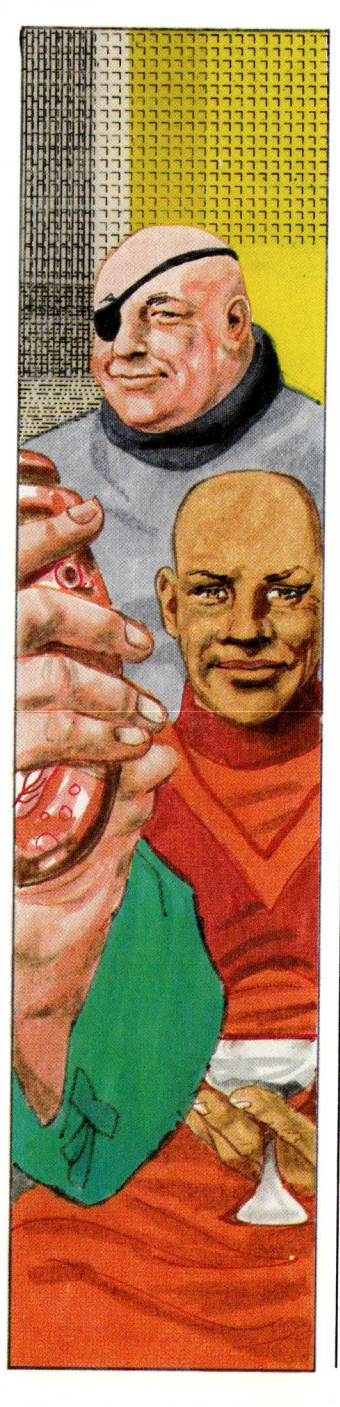

"No," said Benedick. "He is in transit, aboard the *Wallaby*. He had just phased and his mind is still mainly awake. He is running a cargo of ambergris to the Tau Ceti system, fifth planet—Tholmen. After that he plans on vacationing in the Red River Valley of the third planet —Cardiff. Along with the Drillen and the puppy, he has a crewman with him this time. I can't read anything but that it's a retired Guardsman."

"Could *you* be mistaken, Benedick? Reading something, someone else . . . ?"

"No."

"What should we do, Lynx?"—Sandor.

"We should report it"—Lynx.

"Yes."

"It is unfortunate . . . ."

"Yes."

"Tholmen, in Tau Ceti, and he just phased?"—Lynx.

"Yes."

". . . I told you," said the weeping paranorm. "He wasn't ready to die."

There was still some work to be done.

When the *Wallaby* hit Tau Ceti all hell broke loose.

Three fully-manned Guardships, like onto the *Wallaby* herself were waiting.

ICI had quarantined the entire system for three days. There could be no mistaking the ebony toadstool when it appeared on the screen. No identification was solicited.

Corgo prepared to phase again, but it took him forty-three seconds to do so.

During that time he was struck twice by the surviving Guardship.

Then he was gone. Time and chance, which sometimes like to pass themselves off as destiny, then seized upon the *Wallaby*, the puppy, the Drillen, First Mate Emil, and the man without a heart.

Corgo had set no course when he had in-phased. There had been no time. The *Wallaby* jumped blind, and with a broken leg.

Where they had gotten to no one knew, least of all a weeping paranorm who had monitored the battle, despite the continuum-impact and a hangover.

But suddenly Benedick knew fear:

"He's about to phase-out. I'm going to have to drop him now."

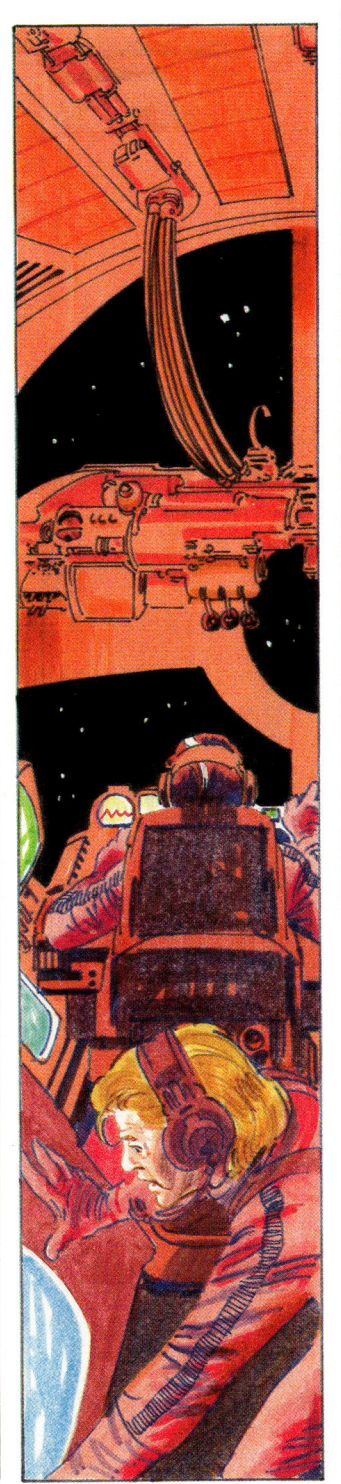

"Do you know where he is?"

"No, of course not!"

"Well, neither does he. Supposing he pops out in the middle of a sun, or in some atmosphere—moving at that speed?"

"Well, supposing he does? He dies."

"Exactly. Continuum-impact is bad enough. I've never been in a man's mind when he died—and I don't think I could take it.

With that he collapsed and could not be roused.

So, Corgo's heart went back into its jar, and the jar went back into the lower right-hand drawer of Sandor's desk, and none of the hunters heard the words of Corgo's answer to his First Mate after the phasing-out:

"Where are we?—The Comp says the nearest thing is a little ping-pong ball of a world called Dombeck, not noted for anything. We'll have to put down there for repairs, somewhere off the beaten track. We need projectors."

So they landed the *Wallaby* and banged on its hull as the hunters slept, some five hundred forty-two miles away.

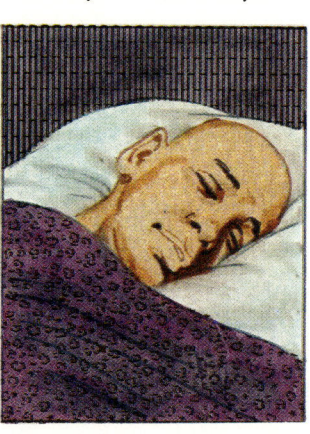

They were grinding out the projector sockets shortly after Sandor had been tucked into his bed.

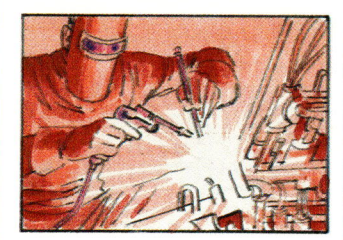

They rewired shorted circuits as Benedick smiled and dreamt of Bright Bad Barby the Bouncing Baby, in the days of her youth.

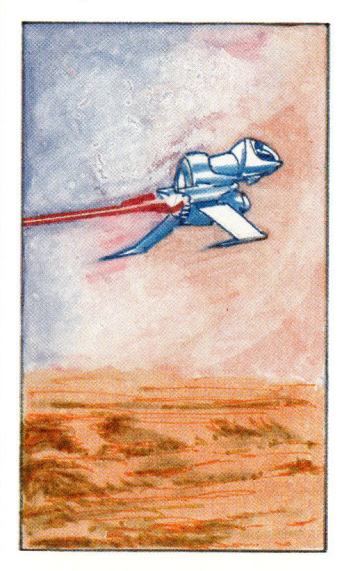

. . . and Corgo took the lightboat and headed for a town three hundred miles away, just as the pale sun of Dombeck began to rise.

"He's here!" cried Benedick, flinging wide the door to the Lynx's room and rushing up to the bedside. "He's—"

Then he was unconscious, for the Lynx may not be approached suddenly as he sleeps.

When he awakened five minutes later, he was lying on the bed and the entire household stood about him. There was a cold cloth on his forehead and his throat felt crushed.

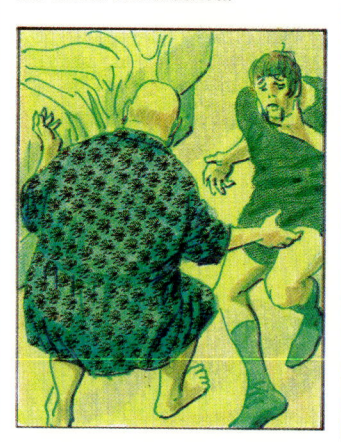

"My brother," said the Lynx, "you should never approach a sleeping man in such a manner."

"B-but he's here," said Benedick, gagging. "Here on Dombeck! I don't even need Sandor to tell!"

"Art sure thou hast not imbibed too much?"

"No, I tell you he's here!" He sat up, flung away the cloth. "That little city, Coldstream—" He pointed through the wall. "—I was there just a week ago. I *know* the place!"

"Then *come* with us to the library and see if you can read it again."

"You better believe I can!"

At that moment Corgo was drinking a cup of coffee and waiting for the town to wake up. He was considering his First Mate's resignation:

"I never wanted to burn anyone, Cap. Least of all, the Guard. I'm sorry, but that's it. No more for me.

Corgo sighed and ordered a second coffee. He glanced at the clock on the diner wall. Soon, soon . . .

"That clock, that wall, that window! It's the diner where I had lunch last week, in Coldstream!" said Benedick, blinking moistly.

"How can we check?"

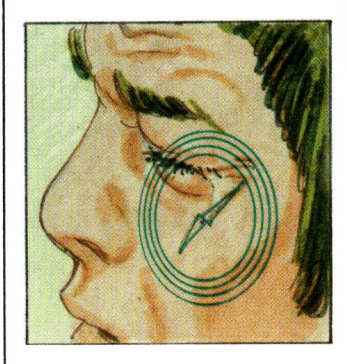

"Call the flamin' diner and ask them to describe their only customer!"—Benedick.

"*That* is a very good idea"—the Lynx.

The Lynx moved to the phone-unit on Sandor's desk.

Sudden, as everything concerning the case had been, was the Lynx's final decision.

"Your flyer, brother Sandor. May I borrow it?"

"Why, yes. Surely . . ."

"I will now call the local ICI office and requisition a laser-cannon. They have been ordered to cooperate with us without question, and the orders are still in effect. It won't take long to mount the gun on your flyer.—Benedick, stay with him every minute now. He still has to buy the equipment, take it back, and install it. Therefore, we should have sufficient time. Just stay with him and advise me as to his movements."

"Check."

"Are you sure it's the right way to go about it?"—Sandor.

"I'm sure . . . ."

As the cannon was being delivered, Corgo made his purchases. As it was being installed, he loaded the lightboat and departed. As it was tested, on a tree stump Aunt Faye had wanted removed for a long while, he was aloft and heading toward the desert.

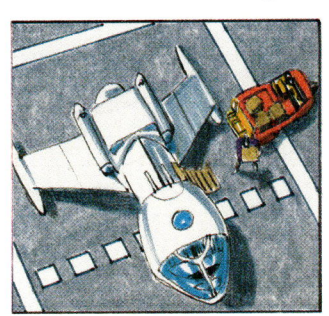

As he crossed the desert, Benedick watched the rolling dunes, scrub-shrubs and darting *rabbophers* through his eyes.

He also watched the instrument-panel.

As the Lynx began his journey, Mala and Dilk were walking about the hull of the *Wallaby*. Mala wondered if the killing was over.

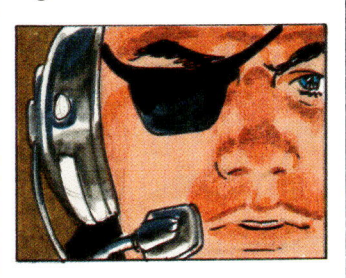

The Lynx maintained radio contact with Benedick. Sandor drank *xmili*. After a time, Corgo landed. The Lynx was racing across the sands from the opposite direction.

They began unloading the light-boat.

The Lynx sped on.

"I am near it now. Five minutes," he radioed back.

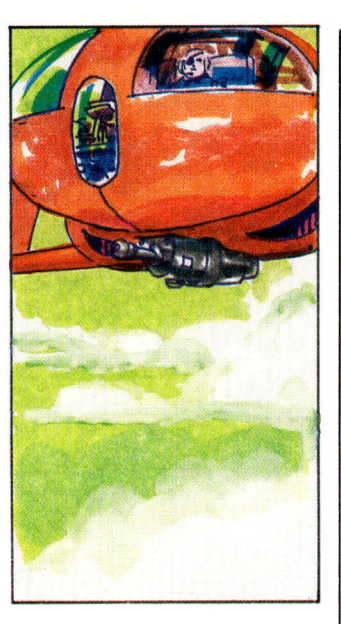

"Then I'm out?"—Benedick.

"Not yet"—the reply.

"Sorry, but you know what I said. I won't be there when he dies."

"All right, I can take it from here"—the Lynx.

Which is how, when the Lynx came upon the scene, he saw a dog and a man and an ugly but intelligent quadraped beside the *Wallaby*.

His first blast hit the ship. The man fell.

The quadraped ran, and he burnt it.

The dog thrashed through the port into the ship.

The Lynx brought the flyer about for another pass.

There was another man, circling around from the other side of the ship, where he had been working.

Corgo's death-ring discharged its single laser beam.

It crossed the distance between them, penetrated the hull of the flyer, passed through the Lynx's left arm above the elbow, and continued on through the roof of the vehicle.

The Lynx cried out, fought the controls, as Corgo dashed into the *Wallaby*.

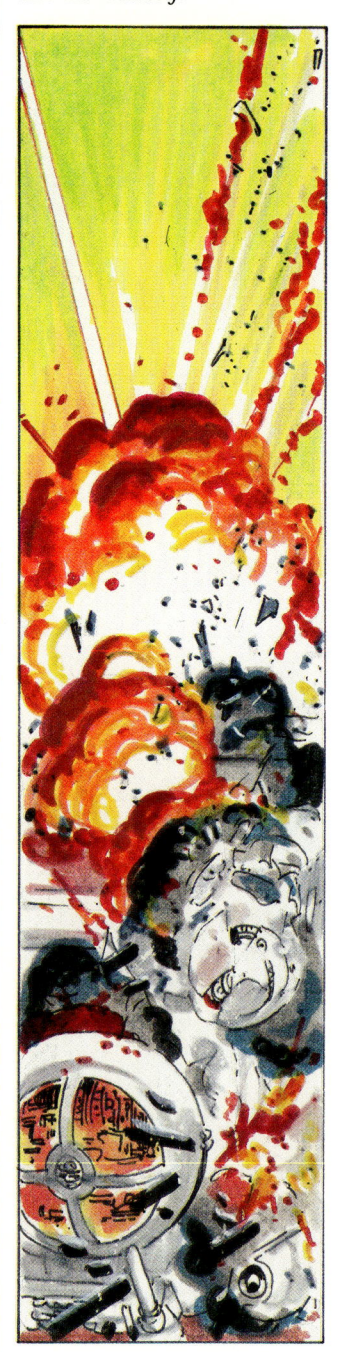

Then he triggered the cannon, and again, and again and again, circling, until the *Wallaby* was a smoldering ruin in the middle of a sea of fused sand.

Still did he burn that ruin, finally calling back to Benedick Benedict and asking his one question.

"Nothing"—the reply.

Then he turned and headed back, setting the autopilot and opening the first-aid kit.

". . . Then he went in to hit the *Wallaby*'s guns, but I hit him first"—Lynx.

"No"—Benedick.

"What meanest thou 'no'? *I* was there."

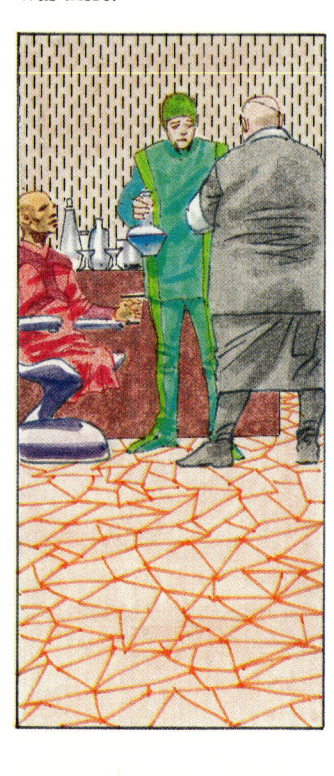

"So was I, for awhile. I *had* to see how he felt."

"And?"

"He went in for the puppy, Dilk, held it in his arms, and said to it, 'I am sorry.' "

"Whatever, he is dead now and we have finished. It is over"—Sandor.

"Yes."

"Yes."

"Let us then drink to a job well done, before we part for good."

"Yes."

"Yes."

And they did.

While there wasn't much left of the *Wallaby* or its Captain, ICI positively identified a synthetic heart found still beating, erratically, amidst the hot wreckage.

Corgo was dead, and that was it.

He should have known what he was up against, and turned himself in to the proper authorities. How can you hope to beat a man who can pick the lock to your mind, a man who dispatched forty-eight men and seventeen malicious alien lifeforms, and a man who knows almost every damn street in the galaxy.

He should have known better than to go up against Sandor Sandor, Benedick Benedict and Lynx Links. He should, he should have known.

For their real names, of course, are Tisiphone, Alecto and Maegaera. They are the furies.

A ZELAZNY TAPESTRY

DOORWAYS IN THE SAND
DAMNATION ALLEY

There are a number of things depicted on the following pages, from such books as *Damnation Alley, Doorways in the Sand,*

Considering them chronologically, *Creatures of Light and Darkness* came first. I had written this book for my own amusement. Thoughts of publication were all afterthoughts. When working in such a fashion, one can be a bit more experimental, and I was. It is a present tense piece, and it includes free verse and a closet drama, among other things. No apologies. It was fun doing it just the way that I did it, and the fact that Larry Ashmead at Doubleday liked it was so much frosting. And thanks again, Chip, for calling it to his attention.

Damnation Alley was a quickly composed, action-adventure piece. No great pretensions here. The fact that it has done as well for me as it has is another dose of frosting. My crusty Hell's Angels protagonist was taken into the back room and worked over more than a bit for the Hollywood version of the story, which basically preserves the title and the special effects. Interested parties can always read the book.

To Die in Italbar represents the only attempt I'd ever made to write a story according to a formula. It was Max Brand's formula, and it sounded good when I heard it: You need two main characters, a good man who goes bad and a bad man who goes good. Their paths cross on their ways up and down. Well...I began the book with every intention of doing that, but partway through I got too interested in the characters as characters, saw an odd tie-in with my earlier novel *Isle of the Dead* and ditched the formula. I sometimes wonder, though, what it would have been like if I hadn't.

Doorways in the Sand represents a great deal of authorial pleasure. It was one of those books that began with a congenial idea, was a fun piece to plot and gave me all sorts of kicks in the writing. Also, the finished product was exactly what I'd desired. They don't all go such a route and turn out this way. *Today We Choose Faces* is one of the few others that moved from conception to paper with hardly a twitch 'twixt ideas and fingertips, perhaps in keeping with the character(s) of the somewhat humorless, singleminded protagonist. About the only things an author can do on discovering he is heir to such good karma are to be thankful and keep on writing. Fred Cassidy, in *Doorways in the Sand*, could, I suppose, be viewed as a metaphor for an author: a perpetual student of anything handy, constantly procrastinating, ever-ready to take advantage of a good thing and willing to go to great lengths and heights for a little solitude. Bon voyage, Titanic...

TODAY WE CHOOSE FACES

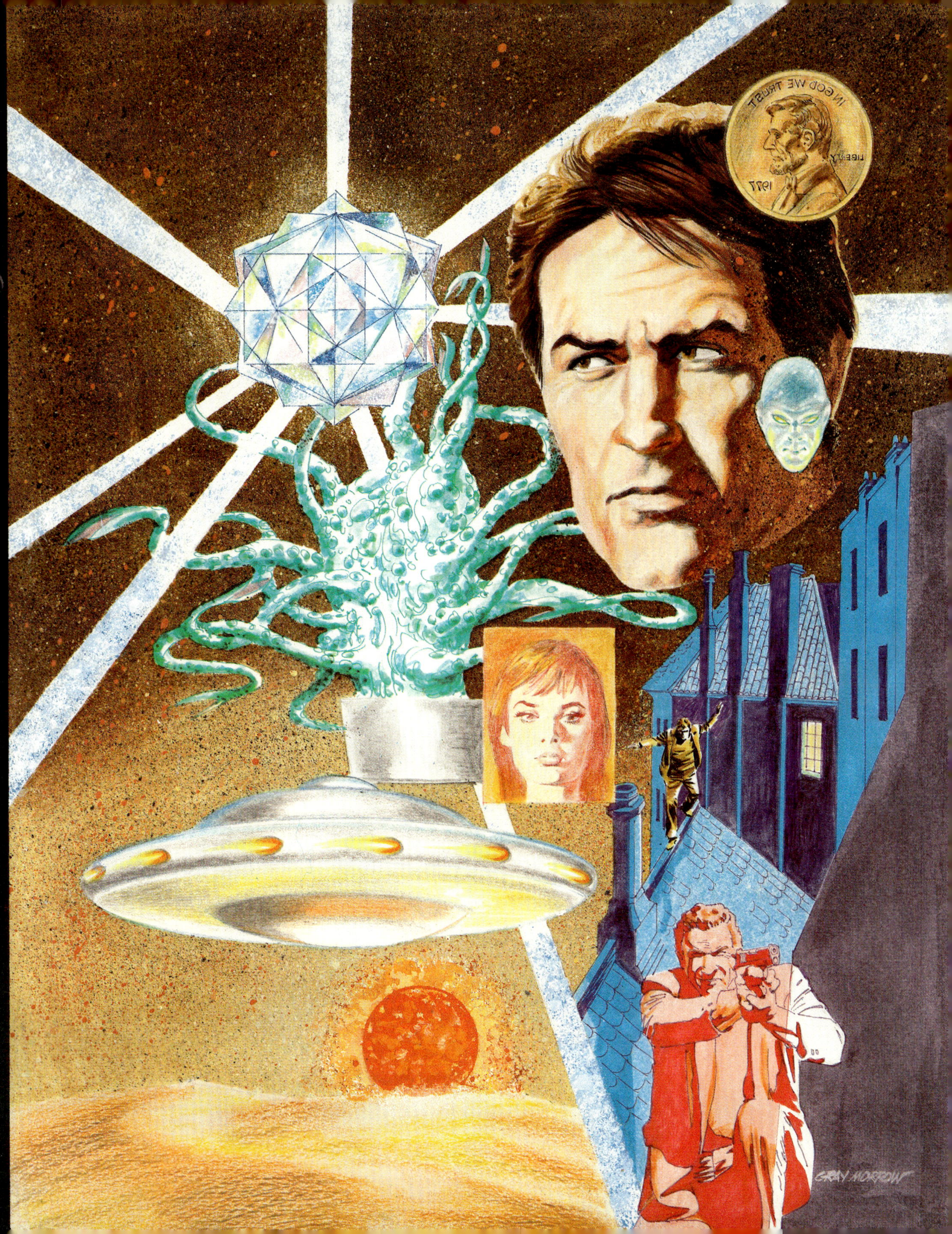
GRAY MORROW

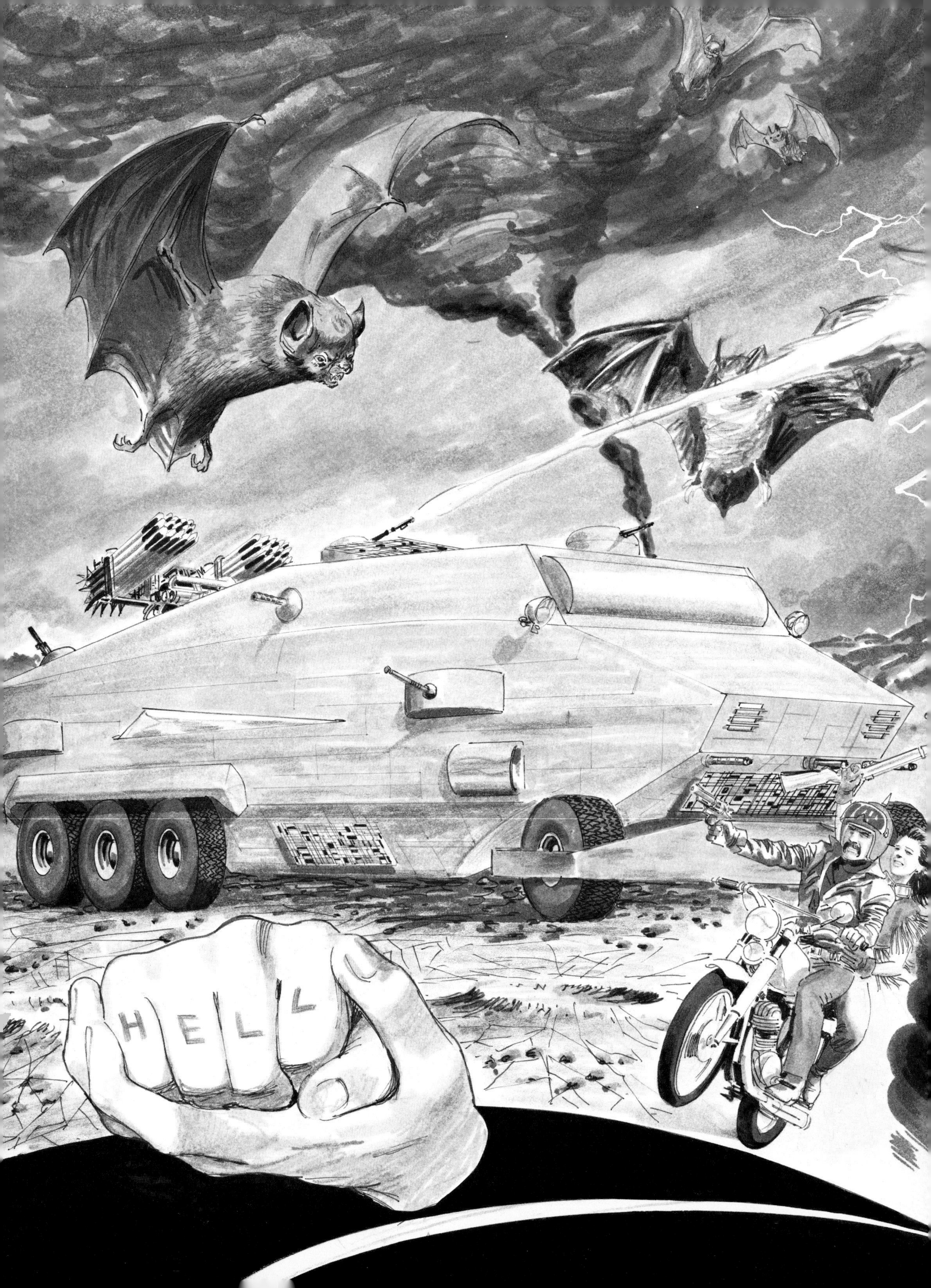
HELL

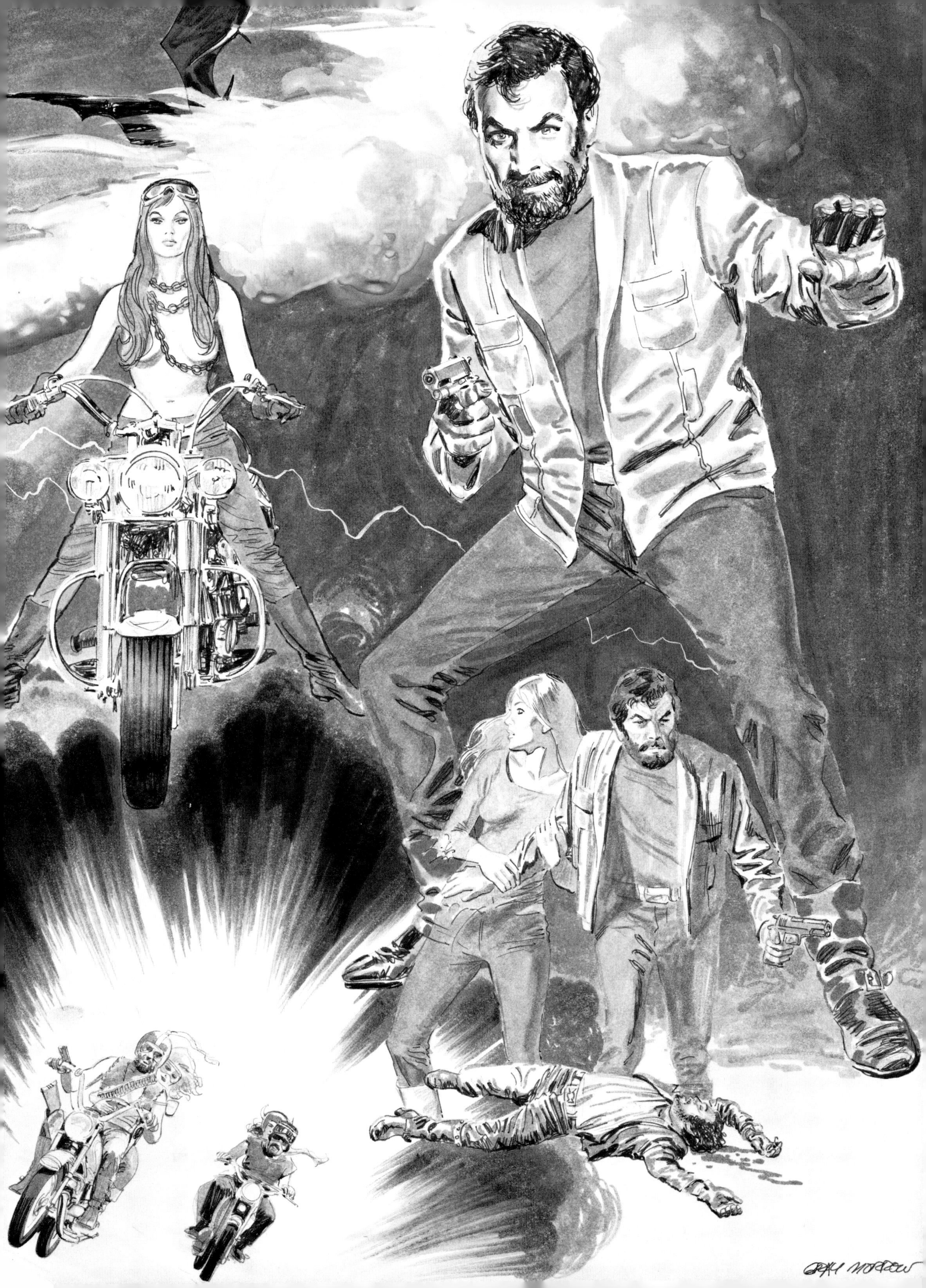
GRAY MORROW

ZELAZNY SPEAKS

First, some comments about the stories in the book not mentioned elsewhere. "The Furies" was an early story, from the period when I was still trying to teach myself about character development. It involves a continuing fascination with the better qualities of bad characters and the worst qualities of good ones, to put it as simply as I can.

"Rock Collector" was a brief experiment of a simple sort. I wanted to do a piece entirely in dialogue. Plot, characters, setting—I wanted them all to emerge simply through talk. By the end, I'd written myself into a corner, though, and I decided that 95% dialogue was sufficient to make for a successful experiment. That's one of the nice things about setting your own goals as a writer. In a pinch, you can always revise them.

I was curious to see how my works would lend themselves to this sort of illustrated adaptation. As I write this, I have not yet seen all of the artwork involved, but what I have seen strikes me as appropriate and impresses me favorably.

I have no desire to define science fiction, and if I ever accidentally come up with what seems a good definition I will attempt to violate it in my next story. I hope to write many more, ranging from pure fantasy through the harder variety of science fiction, and I hope to produce a few interesting hybrids every now and then. Having completed the Amber series, I have begun work on a new novel which I would be happy to plug here, save that I haven't decided on a title yet. It will be the one that begins "Red Dorakeen was on a quiet section of the Road, straight and still as death and faintly sparkling." I hope to see you there.

MORROW SPEAKS

WHAT YOU HOLD IN YOUR HANDS IS AN EXPERIMENT. YEARS AGO, FRIENDS AND I USED TO DAYDREAM ABOUT THE POSSIBILITY OF OUR FAVORITE FANTASY STORIES EVER BEING ACCORDED FULL-SCALE TREATMENTS IN THE VARIOUS MEDIA. "NEVER HAPPEN," WE ALL GRUMPILY AGREED. WELL, HAPPILY WE WERE POOR PROGNOSTICATORS. FILMS LIKE STAR WARS OR CONAN HACKING HIS WAY OUT OF OBSCURITY TO BECOME BIGGER THAN EVER PROVE THAT FACT IS STRANGER THAN EVEN SCIENCE FICTION. WHEN ASKED TO DO THE ILLUSTRATED ZELAZNY, I JUMPED AT THE CHANCE—AND THE CHALLENGE.

HOPEFULLY, YOU, THE READER, WILL FIND THIS BOOK IN SOME MEASURE AS REWARDING AS I DID IN ILLUSTRATING IT. IN ANY CASE, IT HAS BEEN AN EXPERIMENT, AT LEAST FOR ME, WELL WORTH THE DOING.

THE DOORS OF HIS FACE THE LAMPS OF HIS MOUTH

I'm a baitman. No one is born a baitman, except in a French novel where everyone is. (In fact, I think that's the title, *We are All Bait.* Pfft!) How I got that way is barely worth the telling and has nothing to do with neo-exes, but the days of the beast deserve a few words, so here they are.

The Lowlands of Venus lie between the thumb and forefinger of the continent known as Hand. When you break into Cloud Alley it swings its silverblack bowling ball toward you without a warning. You jump then, inside that fire-tailed tenpin they ride you down in, but the straps keep you from making a fool of yourself. You generally chuckle afterwards, but you always jump first.

Next you suck pure oxygen, sigh possibly, and begin the long topple to the Lowlands. There, you are caught like an infield fly at the Lifeline landing area—so named because of its nearness to the great delta in the Eastern Bay—located between the first peninsula and "thumb." For a minute it seems as if you're going to miss Lifeline and wind up as canned seafood, but afterwards—shaking off the metaphors—you descend to scorched concrete and present your middle-sized telephone directory of authorizations to the short, fat man in the gray cap.

The Worlds Almanac re Lifeline: ". . . Port city on the eastern coast of Hand. Employees of the Agency for Non-terrestrial Research comprise approximately 85% of its 100,000 population (2010 Census). Its other residents are primarily personnel maintained by several industrial corporations engaged in basic research. Independent marine biologists, wealthy fishing enthusiasts, and waterfront entrepreneurs make up the remainder of its inhabitants."

I turned to Mike Dabis, a fellow entrepreneur, and commented on the lousy state of basic research.

"Not if the mumbled truth be known."

He paused behind his glass before continuing the slow swallowing process calculated to obtain my interest and a few oaths, before he continued.

"Carl," he finally observed, poker playing, "they're shaping Tensquare."

I could have hit him. I might have refilled his glass with sulfuric acid and looked on with glee as his lips blackened and cracked. Instead, I grunted a noncommital. "Who's fool enough to shell out fifty grand a day? ANR?"

He shook his head. "Jean Luharich, the girl with the violet contacts and fifty or sixty perfect teeth."

"Isn't she selling enough face cream these days?"

He shrugged. "Publicity makes the wheels go 'round. Luharich Enterprises jumped sixteen points when she picked up the Sun Trophy. You ever play golf on Mercury?"

I had, but I overlooked it and continued to press. "So she's coming here with a blank check and a fishhook?"

"*Bright Water*, today," he nodded. "Should be down by now. Lots of cameras. She wants an Ikky, bad."

"Hmm," I hmmed. "How bad?"

"Straight union rates. Triple time for extraordinary circumstances," he narrated. "Be at Hangar Sixteen with your gear, Friday morning, five hundred hours. We push off Saturday, daybreak."

"You're sailing?"

"I'm sailing."

I poured him a drink, concentrating on H_2SO_4, but it didn't transmute. Finally I got him soused and went out into the night to walk and think things over.

Around a dozen serious attempts to land *Ichthyform Leviosaurus Levianthus*, generally known as "Ikky," had been made over the past five years. When Ikky was first sighted, whaling techniques were employed. These proved either fruitless or disastrous, and a new procedure was inaugurated. Tensquare was constructed by a wealthy sportsman named Michael Jandt, who blew his entire roll on the project.

After a year on the Eastern Ocean, he returned to file bankruptcy. Carlton Davits, a playboy fishing enthusiast, then purchased the huge raft and laid a wake for Ikky's spawning grounds. On the nineteenth day out he had a strike and lost one hundred and fifty bills' worth of untested gear, along with one *Ichthyform Levianthus*. Twelve days later, using tripled lines, he hooked, narcotized, and began to hoist the huge beast. It awakened then, destroyed a control tower, killed six men, and worked general hell over five square blocks of Tensquare. Carlton was left with partial hemiplegia and a bankruptcy suit of his own. He faded into waterfront atmosphere and Tensquare changed hands four more times, with less spectacular but equally expensive results.

I've been baitman on three of the voyages, and I've been close enough to count Ikky's fangs on two occasions. I want one of them to show my grandchildren, for personal reasons.

I faced the direction of the landing area and resolved a resolve.

"You want me for local coloring, gal. It'll look nice on the feature page and all that. But clear this—If anyone gets you an Ikky, it'll be me."

I stood in the empty Square. The foggy towers of Lifeline shared their mists.

Venus at night is a field of sable waters. On the coasts, you can never tell where the sea ends and the sky begins. Dawn is like dumping milk into an inkwell. First, there are erratic curdles of white, then streamers. Shade the bottle for a gray colloid, then watch it whiten a little more. All of a sudden you've got day. Then start heating the mixture.

I leaned forward. Feelings played flopdoodle in my guts. I knew every bloody inch of the big raft, but the feelings you once took for granted change when their source is out of reach. Truthfully, I'd had my doubts I'd ever board the hulk again. But now, now I could almost believe in predestination. There it was!

A tensquare football field of a ship. A-powered. Flat as a pancake, except for the plastic blisters in the middle and the "Rooks" fore and aft, port and starboard.

The Rook towers were named for their corner positions—and any two can work together to hoist, co-powering the graffles between them. The graffles—half gaff, half grapple—can raise enormous weights to near water level; their designer had only one thing in mind, though, which accounts for the gaff half. At water level, the Slider has to implement elevation for six to eight feet before the graffles are in a position to push upward, rather than pulling. The Slider, essentially, is a mobile room—a big box capable of moving in any of Tensquare's crisscross groovings and "anchoring" on the strike side by means of a powerful electromagnetic bond.

The Slider houses a section operated control indicator which is the most sophisticated "reel" ever designed. Drawing broadcast power from the generator beside the center blister, it is connected by shortwave with the sonar room, where the movements of the quarry are recorded and repeated to the angler seated before the section control.

The fisherman might play his "lines" for hours, days even, without seeing any more than metal and an outline on the screen. Only when the beast is graffled and the extensor shelf, located twelve feet below waterline, slides out for support and begins to aid the winches, only then does the fisherman see his catch.

We circled till the mechanical flag took notice and waved us on down. We touched beside the personnel hatch and I jettisoned my gear, jumped to the deck and began a tour of Tensquare.

I mounted each Rook, checking out the controls and the underwater video eyes. Then I raised the main lift. Malvern had no objections to my testing things this way. In fact, he encouraged it. We had sailed together before and our positions had even been reversed upon a time. So I wasn't surprised when I stepped off the lift into the Hopkins Locker and found him waiting.

DIAGRAM OF TENSQUARE

"Well, will we fill it?"

I shook my head. "I'd like to, but I doubt it. I don't give two hoots and a damn who gets credit for the catch, so long as I have a part in it. But it won't happen. That gal's an egomaniac. She'll want to operate the Slider, and she can't."

"You ever meet her?"

"Four, five years ago."

"She was a kid then. How do you know what she can do now?"

"I know. She'll have learned every switch and reading by this time. She'll be up on all theory."

"Maybe she can do it, Carl. She's raced torch ships and she's scubaed in bad waters back home."

I ducked through a hatchway. "Maybe you're right, but she was a rich witch when I knew her—and she wasn't *blonde*."

He yawned. "Let's find breakfast."

The screen glowed. I adjusted and got outlines of the bottom. The colors filled the Slider berth.

"Okay."

I threw a Status Blue switch and Dabis matched it. The light went on.

The winch unlocked. I aimed out over the waters, extended the arm, and fired a cast.

"Clean one," he commented.

"Status Red. Call strike." I threw a switch.

"Status Red."

The baitman would be on his way with this, to make the barbs tempting.

It's not exactly a fishhook. The cables bear hollow tubes; the tubes convey enough dope for any army of hopheads; Ikky takes the bait, dandled before him by remote control, and the fisherman rams the barbs home.

My hands moved over the console, making the necessary adjustments. I checked the narco-tank reading. Empty. Good, they hadn't been filled yet. I thumbed the Inject button.

"In the gullet," Mike murmured.

I released the cables. I played the beast imagined. I let him run, swinging the winch to simulate his sweep.

I had the air conditioner on and my shirt off and it was still uncomfortably hot, which is how I knew that morning had gone over its noon. I didn't see Jean arrive or I would have ended the session and gotten below.

She broke my concentration by slamming the door hard enough to shake the bond.

"Mind telling me who authorized you to bring up the Slider?" she asked.

"No one," I replied. "I'll take it below now."

"Just move aside."

I did, and she took my seat. She attacked the panel with a nearly amusing intensity that I found disquieting.

"Status Blue," she snapped, breading a violet fingernail on the toggle.

She worked the winch sideways to show she knew how. I didn't doubt she knew how and she didn't doubt that I didn't doubt, but then—

"In case you're wondering," she said, "you're not going to be anywhere near this thing. You were hired as a baitman, remember? Not a Slider operator! A baitman! Your duties consist of swimming out and setting the table for our friend the monster. It's dangerous, but you're getting well paid for it. Any questions?"

"Nope," I smiled, "but I am qualified to run that thingamajigger—and if you need me I'll be available, at union rates."

"Mister Davits," she said, "I don't want a loser operating this panel."

"Miss Luharich, there has never been a winner at this game."

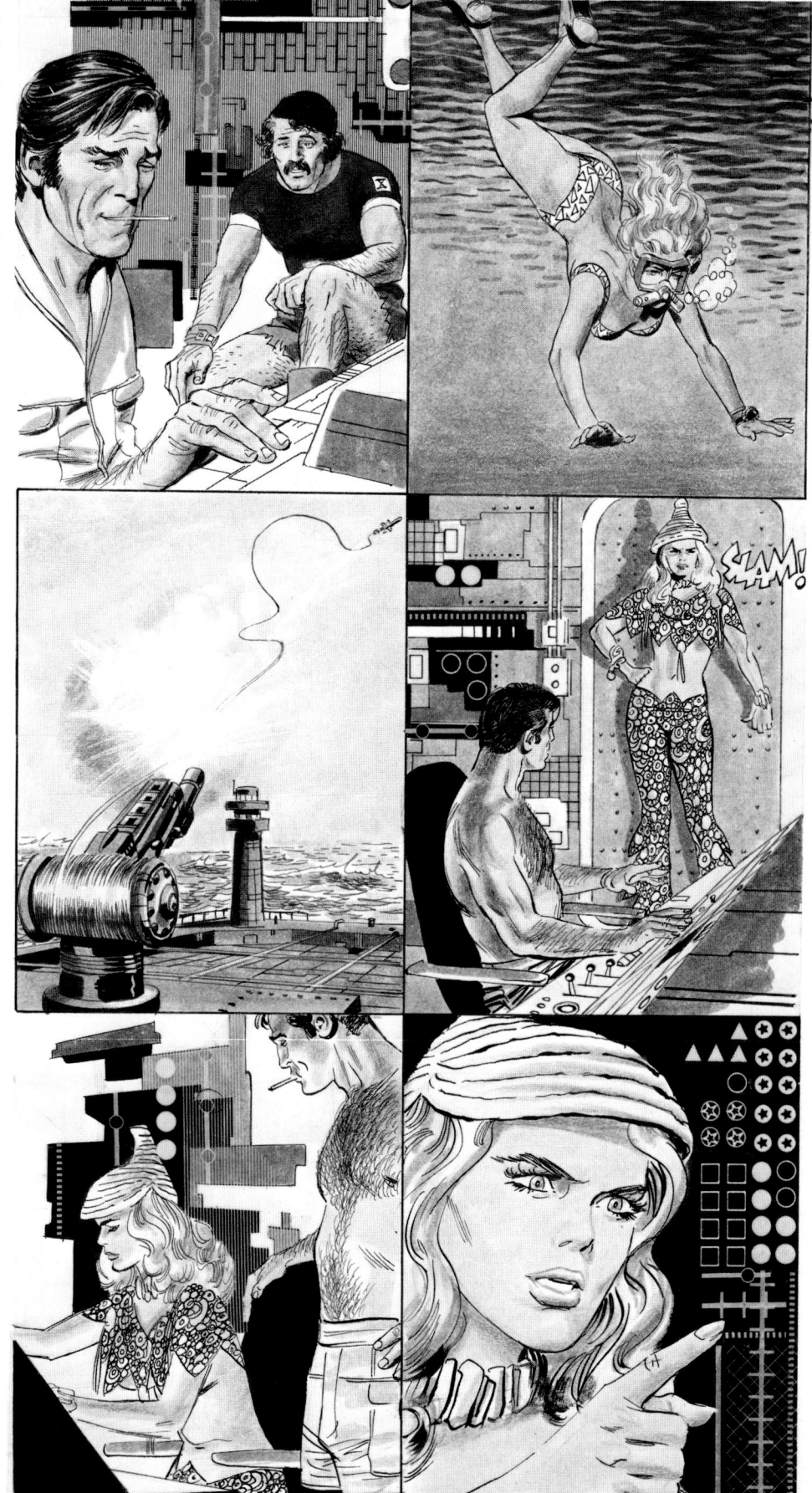

She started reeling in the cable and broke the bond at the same time, so that the whole Slider shook as the big yo-yo returned. We skidded a couple of feet backwards. Slowing, she transferred rails and we jolted to a clanging halt, then shot off at a right angle. The crew scrambled away from the hatch as we skidded onto the elevator.

"In the future, Mister Davits, do not enter the Slider without being ordered," she told me.

"Don't worry. I won't step inside even if I am ordered," I answered. "I signed on as a baitman. Remember? If you want me in here, you'll have to *ask* me."

"That'll be the day," she smiled.

I sat whittling, my legs hanging over the aft edge, the chips spinning down into the furrow of our wake. Three days out. No action.

"You!"

Hair like the end of the rainbow, eyes like nothing in nature, fine teeth.

"Hello."

A delicate curl climbed my knife then drifted out behind us. It settled into the foam and was plowed under. I watched her reflection in my blade, taking a secret pleasure in its distortion.

"Are you baiting me?" she finally asked.

I heard her laugh then, and turned, knowing it had been intentional.

"What, me?"

"I could push you off from here, very easily."

"I'd make it back."

"Would you push me off, then—some dark night, perhaps?"

"They're all dark, Miss Luharich. No, I'd rather make you a gift of my carving."

Solemnly, I passed her the wooden jackass I had been carving. I felt a little sorry and slightly jackass-ish myself, but I had to follow through. I always do. The mouth was split into a braying grin. The ears were upright.

She didn't smile and she didn't frown. She just studied it. "It's very good," she finally said, "like most things you do—and appropriate, perhaps."

"Give it to me." I extended a palm.

She handed it back and I tossed it out over the water. It missed the white water and bobbed for awhile like a pigmy seahorse.

"Why did you do that?"

"It was a poor joke. I'm sorry."

"Maybe you are right, though. Perhaps this time I've bitten off a little too much."

I snorted. "Then why not do something safer, like another race?"

She shook her end of the rainbow. "No. It has to be and Ikky."

"Why?"

"Why did you want one so badly that you threw away a fortune?"

"Man reasons," I said. "An unfrocked analyst once told me, 'Mister Davits, you need to reinforce the image of your masculinity by catching one of every kind of fish in existence.' So I set out to do it. I have one more to go. —Why do you want to reinforce *your* masculinity?"

"I don't," she said. "I don't want to reinforce anything but Luharich Enterprises. My chief statistician once said, 'Miss Luharich, sell all the cold cream and face powder in the System and you'll be a happy girl. Rich, too.'—and he was right. I can look the way I do and do anything, and I sell most of the lipstick and face powder in the System—but I have to be *able* to do anything."

"You do look cool and efficient," I observed.

"I don't feel cool," she said, rising. "Let's get two scuba outfits and I'll race you under Tensquare."

"I'll win, too," she added.

"Daughter of Lir, eyes of Picasso," I said, "you've got yourself a race!"

The surface layer was pleasantly warm. At two fathoms the water was bracing; at five it was nice and cold. At eight we let go the swinging stairway and struck out. Tensquare sped forward and we raced in the opposite direction, tattooing the hull yellow at ten-second intervals.

Beneath us, black. The Mindanao of Venus, where eternity might eventually pass the dead to a rest in cities of unnamed fishes. I twisted my head away and touched the hull with a feeler of light; it told me we were about a quarter of the way along.

I increased my beat to match her stepped-up stroke, and narrowed the distance which she had suddenly opened by a couple meters. She sped up again and I did, too. I spotted her with my beam. She turned and it caught on her mask. I never knew whether she'd been smiling. Probably. She raised two fingers in a V-for-Victory and then cut ahead at full speed.

I should have known. I should have felt it coming. It was just a race to her, something else to win. Damn the torpedoes!

So I leaned into it, hard. I don't shake in the water. Or, if I do it doesn't matter and I don't notice it. I began to close the gap again.

She looked back, sped on, looked back. Each time she looked it was nearer, until I'd narrowed it down to the original five meters.

Then she hit the jatoes. We were about halfway under and she shouldn't have done it. The powerful jets of compressed air could easily rocket her upward into the hull, or tear something loose if she allowed her body to twist. Their main use is in tearing free from marine plants or fighting bad currents. I had wanted them along as a safety measure, because of the big suck-and-pull windmills behind.

She shot ahead like a meteorite, and I could feel a sudden tingle of perspiration leaping to meet and mix with the churning waters.

I swept ahead, not wanting to use my own guns, and she tripled, quadrupled the margin.

The jets died and she was still on course. Okay, I was

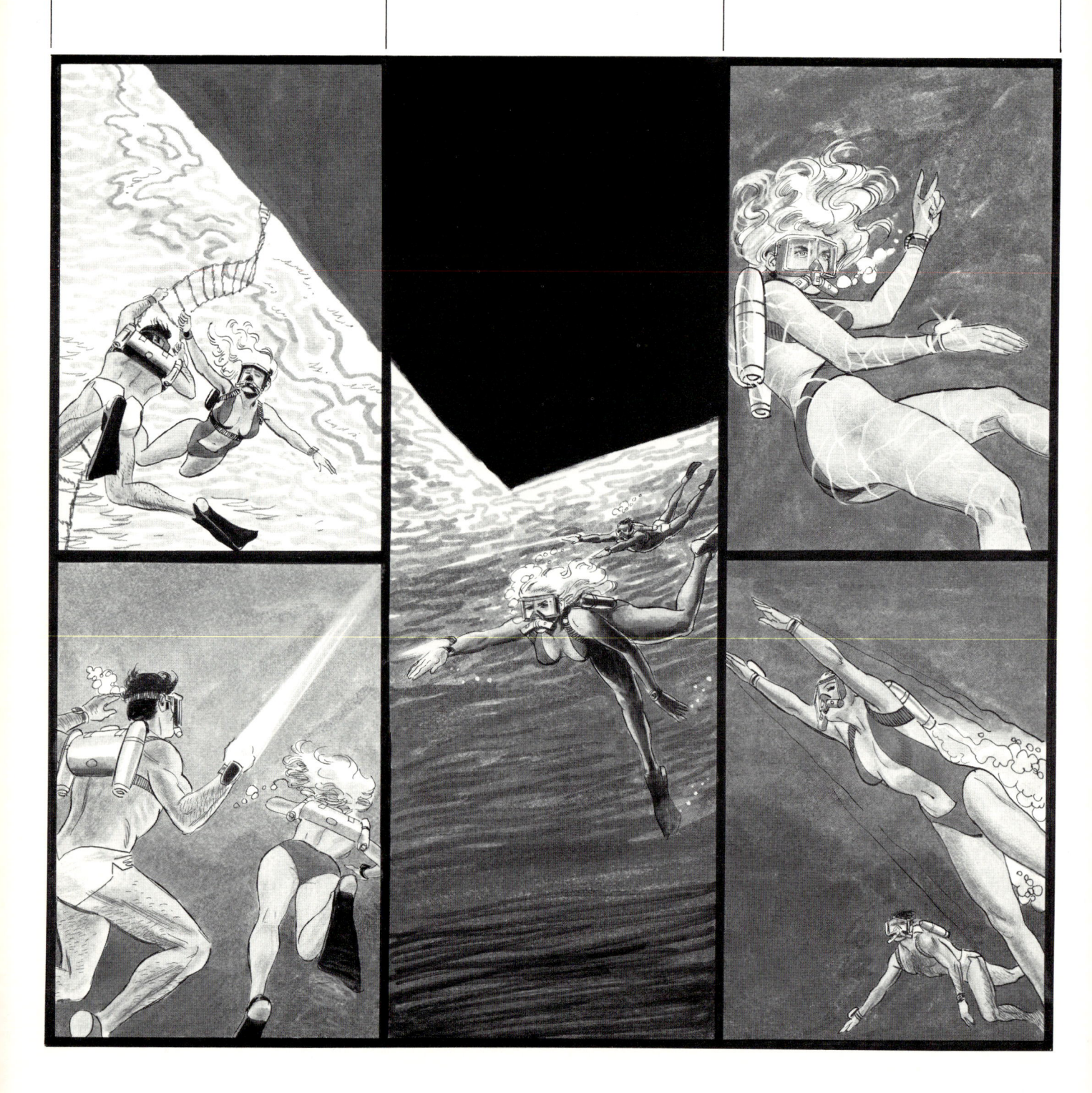

an old fuddyduddy. She *could* have messed up and headed toward the top.

I plowed the sea and began to gather back my yardage, a foot at a time. I wouldn't be able to catch her or beat her now, but I'd be on the ropes before she hit deck.

Then the spinning magnets began their insistence and she wavered. It was an awfully powerful drag, even at this distance. The call of the meat grinder.

She had slowed to half her speed, but she was still moving crosswise, toward the port, aft corner. I began to feel the pull myself and had to slow down. She'd made it past the main one, but she seemed too far back. It's hard to gauge distances under water, but each red beat of time told me I was right. She was out of danger from the main one, but the smaller port screw, located about eighty meters in, was no longer a threat but a certainty.

She had turned and was pulling away from it now. Twenty meters separated us. She was standing still. Fifteen.

Slowly, she began a backward drifting. I hit my jatoes, aiming two meters behind her and about twenty back of the blades.

Straightline! Catching, softbelly, leadpipe on shoulder SWIMLIKEHELL! mask cracked, not broke though AND UP!

We caught a line and I remember brandy.

Into the cradle endlessly rocking I spit, pacing. Insomnia tonight and left shoulder sore again, so let it rain on me—they can cure rheumatism. What I said. In blankets and shivering. She: "Carl, I can't say it." Me: "Then call it square for that night in Govino, Miss Luharich. Huh?" It had only lasted three months. No alimony. Many $ on both sides. Not sure whether they were happy or not. Maybe he should have spent more time on shore. Or perhaps she shouldn't have. Good swimmer, though. Dragged him all the way to Vido to wring out his lungs. Young. Both. Strong. Both. Rich and spoiled as hell. Ditto. Corfu should have brought them closer. Didn't. Many hells. Expensive. He lost a monster or two. She inherited a couple.

The next seventy or eighty thousand waves broke by with a monotonous similarity. The five days that held them were also without distinction. The morning of the thirteenth day out, though, our luck began to rise. The bells broke our coffee-drenched lethargy into small pieces, and we dashed from the galley without hearing what might have been Mike's finest punchline.

"Aft!" cried someone. "Five hundred meters!"

I stripped to my trunks and started buckling. My stuff is always within grabbing distance.

I flipflopped across the deck, girding myself with a deflated squiggler.

"Five hundred meters, twenty fathoms!" boomed the speakers.

The big traps banged upward and the Slider grew to its full height, m'lady at the console. It rattled past me and took root ahead. Its one arm rose and lengthened.

I breasted the Slider as the speakers called, "Four-eighty, twenty!"

"Status Red!"

A belch like an emerging champagne cork and the line arced high over the waters.

"Four-eighty, twenty!" it repeated, all Malvern and static. "Baitman, attend!"

I adjusted my mask and hand-over-handed it down the side. Then warm, then cool, then away.

Green, vast, down. Fast. This is the place where I am equal to a squiggler. If something big decides a bait-man looks tastier than what he's carrying, then irony colors his title as well as the water about it.

I caught sight of the drifting cables and followed them down. Green to dark green to black. It had been a long cast, too long. I'd never had to follow one this far down before. I didn't want to switch on my torch.

But I had to.

Bad! I still had a long way to go. I clenched my teeth and stuffed my imagination into a straightjacket.

Finally the line came to an end.

I wrapped one arm about it and unfastened the squiggler. I attached it, working as fast as I could, and plugged in the little insulated connections which are the reason it can't be fired with the line. Ikky could break them, but by then it wouldn't matter.

My mechanical eel hooked up, I pulled its section plugs and watched it grow. I had been dragged deeper during this operation, which took about a minute and a half. I was near—too near—to where I never wanted to be.

Loathe as I had been to turn on my light, I was suddenly afraid to turn it off. Panic gripped me and I seized the cable with both hands. The squiggler began to glow, pinkly. It started to twist. It was twice as big as I am and doubtless twice as attractive to pink squiggler-eaters. I told myself this until I believed it, then I switched off my light and started up.

If I bumped into something enormous and steel-hided my heart had orders to stop beating immediately and release me—to dart fitfully forever along Acheron, and gibbering.

Ungibbering, I made it to green water and fled back to the nest.

As soon as they hauled me aboard I made my mask a necklace, shaded my eyes, and monitored for surface turbulence. My first question, of course, was: "Where is he?"

"Nowhere," said a crewman; "we lost him right after you went over. Can't pick him up on the scope now. Musta dived."

The squiggler stayed down, enjoying its bath. My job ended for the time being, I headed back to warm my coffee with rum.

Ikky didn't return that day, or that night. We picked up some Dixieland out of Lifeline and let the muskrat ramble while Jean had her supper sent to the Slider. Later she had a bunk assembled inside. I piped in "Deep Water Blues" when it came over the air and waited for her to call up and cuss us out. She didn't, though, so I decided she was sleeping.

Ten hours later someone shook me awake and I propped myself on one elbow, refusing to open my eyes.

"Whassamadder?"

"I'm sorry to get you up," said one of the younger crewmen, "but Miss Luharich wants you to disconnect the squiggler so we can move on."

I knuckled open one eye, still deciding whether I should be amused.

"Have it hauled to the side. Anyone can disconnect it."

"It's at the side now, sir. But she said it's in your contract and we'd better do things right."

"Okay. Run along; tell her I'm on my way—and ask if she has some toenail polish I can borrow."

I'll save on details. It took three minutes in all, and I played it properly, then I went below and made myself a tuna sandwich, with mayonnaise.

Two days like icebergs—bleak, blank, half-melting, all frigid, mainly out of sight, and definitely a threat to peace of mind—drifted by and were good to put behind. I experienced some old feelings.

"*Going shopping?*" asked Mike, who had put a call through for me.

"Going home," I answered.

"Huh?"

"I'm out of the baiting business after this one, Mike. The devil with Ikky! The devil with Venus and Luharich Enterprises! And the devil with you!"

Up eyebrows.

"What brought that on?"

"Five or six things, all added up. The main one being that I don't care any more. Once it meant more to me than anything else to hook that critter, and now it doesn't. I went broke on what started out as a lark and I wanted blood for what it cost me. Now I realize that maybe I had it coming. I'm beginning to feel sorry for Ikky."

"—and you don't want him now?"

"I'll take him if he comes peacefully, but I don't feel like sticking out my neck to make him crawl into the Hopkins."

"I'm inclined to think it's one of the four or five other things you said you added."

"Such as?"

"That look she wears isn't just for Ikky."

"No good, no good." I shook my head. "We're both fission chambers by nature. You can't have jets on both ends of the rocket and expect to go anywhere—what's in the middle just gets smashed."

"That's how it *was*. None of my business, of course—"

"She doesn't care about that bloody reptile, she came here to drag you back where you belong. You're not the baitman this trip."

"Five years is too long."

"There must be something under that cruddy hide of yours that people like," he muttered, "or I wouldn't be talking like this."

"Buddy," I chuckled, "do you know what I'm going to do when I hit Lifeline?"

"I can guess."

"You're wrong. I'm torching it to Mars, and then I'll cruise back home, first class. Venus bankruptcy provisions do not apply to Martian trust funds, and I've still got a wad tucked away where moth and corruption enter not. I'm going to pick up a big old mansion on the Gulf and if you're ever looking for a job you can stop around and open bottles for me."

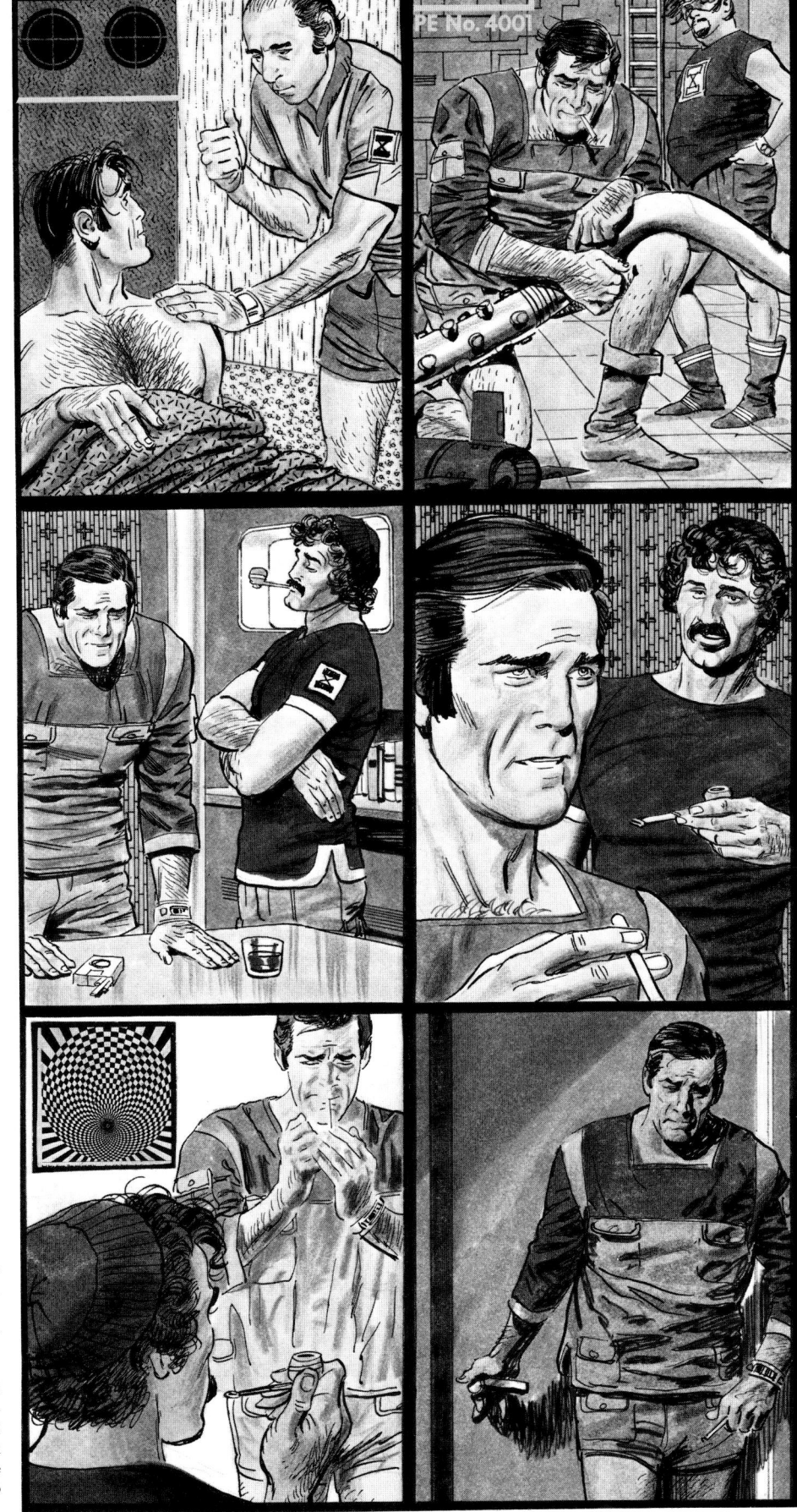

"I've heard the stories about you both," he said. "So you're a heel and a goofoff and she's a bitch. That's called compatibility these days. I dare you, baitman, try keeping something you catch."

I turned. "If you ever want that job, look me up."

I closed the door quietly behind me and left him sitting there waiting for it to slam.

The day of the beast dawned like any other. Two days after my gutless flight from empty waters I went down to rebait. Nothing on the scope. I was just making things ready for the routine attempt.

I hollered a "good morning" from outside the Slider and received an answer from inside before I pushed off. I had reappraised Mike's words, sans sound, sans fury, and while I did not approve of their sentiment or significance, I had opted for civility anyhow.

So down, under, and away. I followed a decent cast about two hundred-ninety meters out. The snaking cables burned black to my left and I paced their undulations from the yellowgreen down into the darkness. Soundless lay the wet night, and I bent my way through it like a cock-eyed comet, bright tail before.

I caught the line, slick and smooth, and began baiting. An icy world swept by me then, ankles to head.

It was a draft, as if someone had opened a big door beneath me. I wasn't drifting downwards that fast either. Which meant that something might be moving up. Something big enough to displace a lot of water. I still didn't think it was Ikky. A freak current of some sort, but not Ikky. Ha!

I had finished attaching the leads and pulled the first plug when a big, rugged, black island grew beneath me. . . .

I flicked the beam downward. His mouth was opened.

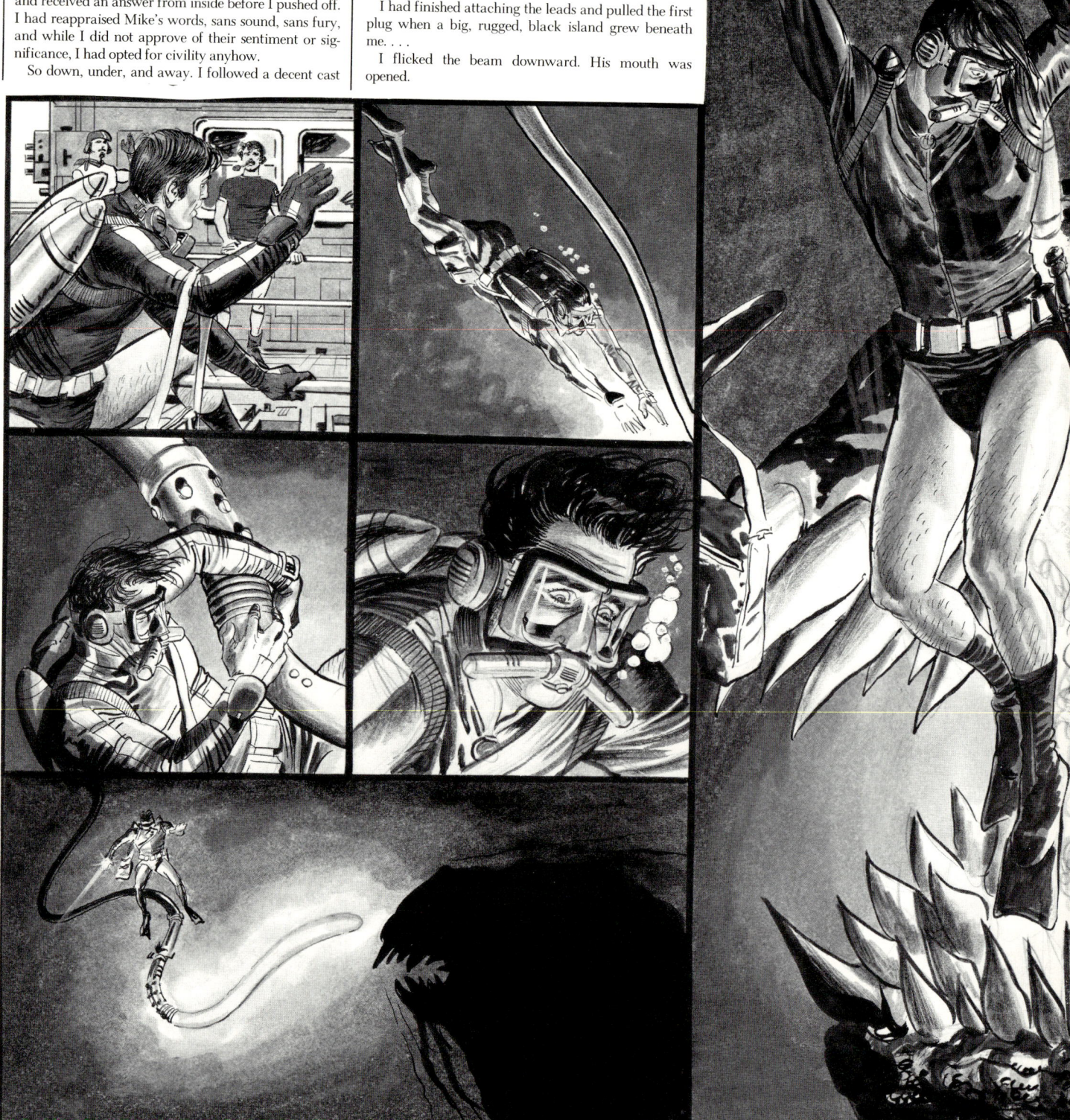

I was rabbit.

Waves of the death-fear passed downward. My stomach imploded. I grew dizzy.

Thing left to do. I managed it, finally. I pulled the rest of the plugs.

I could count the scaly articulations ridging his eyes by then.

The squiggler grew, pinked into phosphorescence . . . squiggled!

A glance back as I jammed the jatoes to life.

He was so near that the squiggler reflected on his teeth, in his eyes. Four meters, and I kissed his lambent jowls with two jets of backwash as I soared. Then I didn't know whether he was following or had halted. I began to black out as I waited to be eaten.

The jatoes died and I kicked weakly.

Too fast, I felt a cramp coming on. One flick of the beam, cried rabbit. One second, to know . . .

Or end things up, I answered. No, rabbit, we don't dart before hunters. Stay dark.

Green waters finally, to yellowgreen, then top.

Doubling, I beat off toward Tensquare. The waves from the explosion behind pushed me on ahead. The world closed in, and a screamed, "He's alive!" in the distance.

A giant shadow and a shock wave. The line was alive, too. Happy Fishing Grounds. Maybe I did something wrong. . . .

Somewhere Hand was clenched. What's bait?

Someone was shaking me. Gloom and cold. Spotlights bled yellow on the deck. I was in a jury-rigg bunk, bulked against the center blister. Swaddled wool, I still shivered.

"It's been eleven hours. You're not going to see anything now."

I tasted blood.

"Drink this."

Water. I had a remark but I couldn't mouth it.

"How long since last time he showed?"

"Two hours, about."

"Jean?"

"She won't let anyone in the Slider. Listen, Mike says come on in. He's right behind you in the blister."

I sat up and turned. Mike was watching. He gestured; I gestured back.

I got to my feet and made it into the blister.

"Howza gut?" queried Mike.

I checked the scope. No Ikky. Too deep.

"You buying?"

"Yeah, coffee." He poured.

"You do that well. Been practicing for that job?"

"What job?"

"The one I offered you—"

A blot on the scope!

"Rising, ma'am! Rising!" he yelled into the box.

"Thanks, Mike. I've got it in here," she crackled.

"Jean!"

"Shut up! She's busy!"

"Was that Carl?"

"Yeah," I called. "Talk later," and I cut it.

Why did I do that?

"Why did you do that?"

I didn't know.

"I don't know."

Damned echoes! I got up and walked outside.

Nothing. Nothing.

Something?

Tensquare actually rocked! He must have turned when he saw the hull and started downward again. White water to my left, and boiling. An endless spaghetti of cable roared hotly into the belly of the deep.

I stood awhile, then turned and went back inside.

Two hours sick. Four, and better.

"The dope's getting to him."

"Yeah."

"What about Miss Luharich?"

"She signed the contract for this. She knew what might happen. It did."

"I think you could land him."

"So do I."

"So does she."

"Then let her ask me."

Ikky was drifting lethargically, at thirty fathoms.

I took another walk and happened to pass behind the Slider. She wasn't looking my way.

"Carl, come in here!"

Eyes of Picasso, that's what, and a conspiracy to make me Slide . . .

"Is that an order?"

"Yes—No! Please."

"Don't ask how I feel," I croaked. "I know that comes next, but don't ask me. Okay?"

"Okay. Want to go below now?"

"No. Just get me my jacket."

"Right here."

"What's he doing?"

"Nothing. He's deep, he's doped but he's staying down."

I dashed inside and monitored. He was rising.

"Push or pull?"

I slammed the "wind" and he came like a kitten.

"Make up your own mind now."

He balked at ten fathoms.

"Play him?"

"No!"

She wound him upwards—five fathoms, four . . .

She hit the extensors at two, and they caught him. Then the graffles.

The crew saw Ikky.

He began to struggle. She kept the cables tight, raised the graffles . . . Up.

Another two feet and the graffles began pushing.

Screams and fast footfalls. Giant beanstalk in the wind, his neck, waving. The green hills of his shoulders grew.

"He's big, Carl!" she cried.

He grew, and grew, and grew uneasy . . .

"Now!"

"Now!"

"I can't!"

It was going to be so damnably simple this time, now the rabbit had died. I reached out.

I stopped.

"Push it yourself."

"I can't. You do it. Land him, Carl!"

"No. If I do, you'll wonder for the rest of your life whether you could have. I know you will, because we're alike, and I did it that way. Find out now!"

She stared.

I gripped her shoulders.

"Could be that's me out there," I offered. "I am a green sea serpent, a monstrous beast, and out to destroy you. I am answerable to no one. Push the Inject."

Her hand moved to the button, jerked back.

"Now!"

She pushed it.

I lowered her still form to the floor and finished things up with Ikky.

It was a good seven hours before I awakened to the steady, sea-chewing grind of Tensquare's blades.

"You're sick," commented Mike.

"How's Jean?"

"The same."

"Where's the beast?"

"Here."

"Good." I rolled over: ". . . Didn't get away this time."

So that's the way it was. No one is born a baitman, I don't think, but the rings of Saturn sing epithalamium the sea-beast's dower.

ROCK COLLECTOR

"YOU CAN'T. I CHECKED YOUR MASS. IT'LL TAKE AT LEAST EIGHT MONTHS UNDER EARTH'S CONDITIONS FOR YOU TO REACH DEEBLING SIZE."

"HAVE YOU NO COMPASSION? I'VE ADDED SO CAREFULLY TO MY ATOM COLLECTION, BUILDING UP THE FINEST MOLECULAR STRUCTURE. NOW, TO BE SNATCHED AWAY RIGHT BEFORE DEEBLING TIME— IT'S UNROCK OF YOU."

"IT'S NOT THAT BAD. I PROMISE YOU THE FINEST EARTH ATOMS AVAILABLE."

"SMALL CONSOLATION! I WANT ALL MY FRIENDS TO SEE."

THE FACT THAT IT WAS A SHORT-JAUNT SPORT MODEL SEDAN, CUSTOMIZED BY IT'S OWNER, WHO HAD REMOVED MUCH OF THE SHIELDING, WAS THE REASON STONE FELT A SUDDEN FLUSH OF VOLCANIC DRUNKENESS, RAPIDLY ADDED SELECT ITEMS TO HIS COLLECTION AND DEEBLED ON THE SPOT!

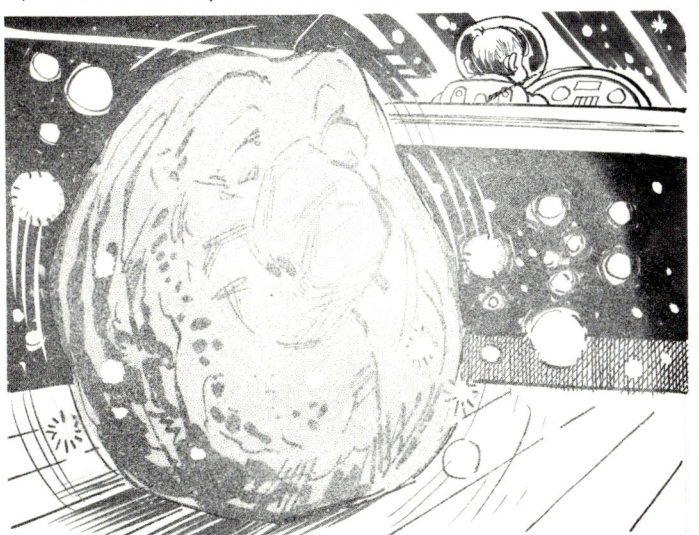

"GONE FISSION-- AND SOONER THAN WE EXPECTED!"

"AN EXCELLENT DEEBLE! IT ALWAYS PAYS TO BE A CAUTIOUS COLLECTOR!"

FINIS

ABOUT THE CONTRIBUTORS

Author Roger Zelazny

Roger Zelazny is one of America'a foremost writers of fantasy. His novels include, *Doorways in the Sand, Jack of Shadows, Today We Choose Faces, ...And Call Me Conrad, The Dreammaker, Creatures of Light and Darkness, Isle of the Dead, Damnation Alley, Lord of Light,* and the *Amber Series—Guns of Avalon, The Hand of Oberon, Nine Princes in Amber, Sign of the Unicorn.*

Among his most prominent short stories are *A Rose for Ecclesiastes, This Moment of this Storm, The Doors of His Face, the Lamps of His Mouth* and *Home is the Hangman.* Three collections of his short fantasy have appeared—*Four for Tomorrow, My Name is Legion* and *Doors of His Face, Lamps of His Mouth.*

His work is distinctive within the literature of fantasy for its relationship to Arthurian lore, classical mythology, theology, philosphy, Celtic legend and arcetypal pulp s.f.

Roger Zelazny is an entertainer, a first-rate storyteller who infuses his writing with rousing adventure and an engaging narrative drive. He is one of the most successful writers in the field of science fiction, a Nebula-and-Hugo-award-winning alumni of the experimental sixties. An adaptation of his *Damnation Alley* made a lucrative but unimpressive tour of American theatres in 1977. He is currently working on a new novel.

Of his work, Roger says, "I write s.f. for love and money. I have been doing it for 15 years, the first 7 on a part-time basis. Most science fiction writers are concerned with the history of ideas. They like to read and talk and daydream and call it research when somebody asks them what they're doing. To justify it beyond this and to pay their bills, they tailor some of the dreams and put them down on paper."

Illustrator Gray Morrow

An artist with a long record of experience in almost every aspect of the commercial illustration field, Gray Morrow made his professional debut in the pages of old pulp and comics magazines. He produced numerous stories for the Atlas and AG comics groups, then moved on to paperback and magazine covers for such titles as *Galazy* and *If.*

Lucrative magazine and illustration work followed. In the sixties, he became one of the most popular and widely seen science fiction cover artists. By the seventies, Gray's work as a humorist appeared frequently in the pages of *National Lampoon,* for whom he produced a short but memorable series of "Great Moments in Humor."

For Ace Books he painted a record 100 *Perry Rhodan* covers. Interim fantasy assignments included a Star Trek poster, short stories for National and Warren magazines and *Orior* for *Witzend.*

From the comic strip medium Gray has illustrated *Flash Gordon, Mandrake, Prince Valiant, Captain America, the Vigilante* and a color folio of classic characters, "Heroes." A book of his sketches entitled "Dark Domain" was published in 1970.

Gray's versatility and style is known throughout the New York illustration scene. From his painting of Cordwainer Smith's *Nostrilia* to his drawings for *Esquire,* his work has been applauded for both its realism and technique. He currently pursues a multipicty of careers, as cartoonist for *Big Ben Bolt,* poster artist and graphic story illustrator for *Heavy Metal* magazine.

Editor/Adaptor Byron Preiss

Producer of numerous experimental books of science fiction and fantasy, Preiss' background rests in both the publishing and electronic communications fields. He has been a writer for ABC-TV, producer/director of short films and editor at the Children's Television Workshop in New York.

His series *Fiction Illustrated* and *Weird Heroes* earned him special recognition from graphic story fans in San Diego and England. His work with Ralph Reese, *ONE YEAR AFFAIR* was published as a collection by Workman Publishing. He has written graphic story material based on Piri Thomas' classic *Down These Mean Streets* and is currently producing a special illustrated version of Theodore Sturgeon's work with Alex Nino and a writer Doug Moench.

A resident of New York, he says of the *Illustrated Zelazny,* "It takes the concept of adapatation into illustrated form one step further. By using a variety of design structures to express the movement and enviroments of Roger's stories, this book expands the realm of what a "comic" can be. This is more than a book of stories, it is an experiment by some very talented people. I am especially grateful to Gray Morrow, (and Mike Goldin and Steve Oliff) for their tremendous work on the illustrations for the book."